# Weeds and Flowers

## By Michelle Garren Flye

This book is dedicated to the wonderful authors and editors of Zoetrope.com who make books like these a reality. Special thanks to Steve Gullion and Kathy Fish who read and critiqued a large portion of this book. Thank you all!

**Praise for Weeds and Flowers:**

"…a wonderful story that makes you stop and think. It's about love, loss, and life. So well written it makes you feel like you were there, seeing all with your own eyes."
-- *Booked Up Reviews*

**5 stars on Amazon:**

"Gripping…Couldn't put it down til the end...and then wanted to read more about them."

"Great Read!!...I loved this from start to finish!!"

"Loved This Story!... I loved the main character and I thought the story was very realistic. I didn't want the book to end."

# Preface

I originally wrote *Weeds and Flowers* in bits and pieces of flash and micro fiction inspired by events, feelings and memories of my childhood. When I took these bits and pieces and began to stitch them together into my first novel, it was like one of those crazy quilts that our grandmothers used to put together out of the scraps from the scrap bag. My friends from the online writing site Zoetrope.com (see the dedication) helped me smooth the mess out and create a more cohesive storyline, like a quilt with an actual pattern.

This story is very special to me. Although it was inspired by an actual, very tragic event in my small hometown in the early 1980s, it is not true. I like to call it a "true fiction" story, though. Although none of it ever happened, it's based on a smidgeon of fact.

For those who were involved in the horrific event that inspired my story, I do not consider this novel an attempt to tell your story. This is my story, based on amorphous memories from my childhood. None of the people in this story ever existed, the murder and trial I describe never happened. But if you look below the events related, that's where you'll find the truth I remember.

In the shadows…

# Chapter One

This is a ghost story. Some of the ghosts are even real.

Shadows fill the garden at this time of year. In a few weeks, the daffodils will spring through the black, mulchy earth and the dogwoods will sprout white and pink crosses on their bare limbs, brightening the darker areas and casting new shadows on softer places.

But in this muddy pre-spring time, the bare branches spread hard shadows on barren muddy ground that swells with secrets not quite ready to be revealed.

Jeff sits on the gray bench next to me. His voice sounds like the wind in the bare branches. "Charlie, do you remember--"

"I remember," I say and we are quiet.

In my dream, the lawnmower glides across the green stretch of grass that leads to the garden. It spits out flecks of emerald. At the perimeter of the garden, the flecks change and amethyst mixes with the emerald, and I know the lawnmower is chewing up the iris border. The lawnmower never slows as it enters the garden. The picket fence becomes splinters of white and brown. The grapevine spews out as a muddy fluid. Then the lawnmower moves into the rose garden, but the cloud of debris isn't red and yellow and white and pink like the roses. Instead, the confetti the lawnmower kicks up is black. Then everything goes black, and I wake.

The only place I know of with no shadows is the beach at noon on a sunny day. Whenever possible, this is where I am when I call my mother. A place with no shadows has no shades of gray.

"How's David?" I study the sparkling ocean.

She's hundreds of miles away in my hometown in the mountains of North Carolina, but she sounds like she's sitting right next to me. "He's…fine." She hesitates just a little, enough to let me know he's not fine, it sucks what's happened to him and I suck for not being there. For him. For her. "How are the wedding plans?" She speaks in a bright voice. She's being a martyr, determined not to bring me down with her troubles.

I roll my eyes and reach for patience. I'm not sure when Mom started rewriting my childhood, but at some point walks down memory lane with her became as dangerous as marching through a minefield. Things I remembered, was sure of in fact, she denied ever happened. Most times she replaced my memories with storybook occurrences. Trips to the zoo, melting ice cream cones, greeting the mailman at the door with a plate full of cookies. Maybe my childhood wasn't bad, but I certainly never could've claimed such a perfect childhood as she "remembered."

In fact, when I think of my childhood, I think of weeds and flowers, sun-drenched color and shadowy spaces. In college, I took a biology class that studied the many flora and fauna of the rainforest. The pictures in my textbook closely resembled the childhood impressions in my mind. Secret things I had never looked at too closely. That was what gardens were and always will be to me--lovely flowers on the surface, weeds encroaching beneath and dark spaces in between. Snakes twined in a grapevine and beetles crouching under decorative borders of violets. If I strolled casually through the garden of my memories, I saw only the beautiful flowers, the happy times. However, if I stopped to look at any particular memory closely, or if I stooped to look underneath, the underlying blackness encroached.

But David is a bright flower in my memory garden, even back then. On their first date, Mom left me with a sitter, but they were back by nine. David talked my mom into taking me to Dairy Queen for an ice cream sundae. I fell in love with him as I sat in my pajamas in the back of his Plymouth Duster and he ate his ice cream and leaned over the bench seat to include me in the conversation.

"I wish you'd come home." Mom sounds plaintive. "Just for a little while, sweetheart."

I close my eyes. Even closed, I can see a rosy glow of the warm sun, but I know the dark is coming.

David was wonderful. Always. But the year he married my mother started a string of changes for me. The spring I turned twelve, my mom had a "change-of-life" baby. I would come home from school to find them asleep on the couch together, the shades drawn. I would get myself a snack and do my homework while they slept, and then, if they were still sleeping, I would go outside and throw sticks at the turtles in the pond. I'm sure I felt my life had changed dramatically from what it had been when it was the two of us. I'm not sure anymore if my own memory is correct about how I felt about it. I suppose all our memory banks stop working properly after a while.

## Chapter Two

"Sweetheart, you want to say goodbye to your mom?" The hall light outlined David, turning him from man into silhouette. "I'm taking her to the hospital now."

The kitchen light spilled into the darkened living room. The digital clock on the mantel read three thirty-two AM. Mom sat on the couch, breathing three short breaths at a time like they taught her in the childbirth class she and David and I went to. Mom had wanted me to attend the labor, too, telling David a teenage girl was plenty old enough. David insisted they ask me, though, and I admitted I didn't want to go. So they made arrangements with my old babysitter Julie to be on call near the baby's due date.

"Hi, Sweetie." Mom held her hand out to me. I took it but didn't sit down. Mom was so tense, it seemed the slightest jarring would be painful for her. Looking at her swollen belly, I felt, as I had many times over the past nine months, that somebody else had swallowed my mother. As if she were now Not-My-Mom. And soon she would be somebody else's mother.

"Everything's fine. I've been through this before, after all." She touched my face with a gentle hand, but the fingers curled in pain, and she began the short, sharp breaths again.

"David! I think you should hurry." I was worried, but I also sensed that I wanted to not have to watch this. I wanted David to take her away so I wouldn't have to see her so vulnerable.

Julie stood next to me on the porch, her heavy arm around my shoulders as David led Mom down the sidewalk, opened the passenger door of his new Lincoln and helped her in. The headlights swept across us as he backed down the driveway, then the taillights disappeared like two red fireflies.

I spent the rest of the night wrapped in my favorite blanket, the one I had back when my real father lived with us. My fingers picked at the frayed edges until I heard Julie in the kitchen scrambling eggs and frying bacon. Then I called my best friend Marleen Galloway. Her brother Kyle answered. Kyle worked at Sound of the Beat, the record store in town. Kyle was planning to go to college next year, not like Marleen's other brother, Jeff. Jeff was fourteen, but he'd only be in the eighth grade next year, and he didn't have a job.

"Sure, I'll wake her up, Charlie." Kyle sounded so kind and understanding when I explained why I was calling so early. "Hang in there. Your mom'll be fine."

"Charlie? Whaszhup?" Marleen's voice still sounded foggy. In the summer, Marleen never got up before ten o'clock. For that matter, neither did I, usually. Still, I needed my best friend, and it didn't take much to convince Marleen of the importance of my situation.

"I'll be over in an hour," she said.

I hung up, wrapped my blanket around my shoulders like a shawl and went downstairs. Julie was already at the table, eating eggs and bacon. "Good morning." She smiled and motioned to another plate. She'd left the morning paper beside it. I'd been reading the morning paper since I was seven years old, and Julie, like all good babysitters, remembered. I nibbled at a piece of toast. Julie made toast in the oven under the broiler, and she put pats of butter on the upper side. Five of them, and they left little squares of yellow on the brown surface of the toast. Normally I love Julie's toast. Today, I could barely swallow.

"Not hungry?" Julie smiled and patted my hand.

I shook my head. I picked up the newspaper and looked at the headlines but didn't open it.

"Your mom's going to be fine," Julie said.

"Yeah." I nodded.

"Really."

"Yeah." I pretended to read.

The doorbell rang and I jumped up and headed to the door, the ragged blanket still clutched around my shoulders. It was Marleen. She shook her head at the sight of me. Marleen liked to pretend to be older than 12. In her mind, we were both grownups already.

"You look like hell," she said.

"Language." Julie frowned from the kitchen door.

"You look bad." Marleen looked at Julie who nodded and let the kitchen door swing shut. Marleen shot a bird at the closed door.

We went upstairs after I caught Julie in the kitchen checking the phone to make sure it was working. I'm sure she thought I hadn't noticed, but I did. It was 8:30, and we hadn't heard from Mom or David.

I led Marleen into the nursery. David had painted it yellow and I had helped Mom hang the painted white ducks and the pink, blue and yellow ABC on the wall more than a month ago. Marleen and I lay on the floor next to the new white crib. Everything in the room smelled new. Mom had sold all the baby stuff she used for me a long time ago, probably thinking she'd never need it again. I doubted I'd had anything so nice when I was a baby, anyway.

"So, do you think anything's wrong?" Marleen looked at the duck mobile above the crib instead of at me. I didn't think anything was wrong, but I wished she hadn't asked the question anyway.

"Nah, what could be wrong?" I propped my feet on the crib and traced each rail with the tip of my toe. "She's fine, right? I mean, she's been through this before."

Marleen looked at me and shook her head. "I dunno, Charlie. Your mom's not exactly as young as she was when she had you. She's twelve years older now."

"She's 36," I said. "Women have babies right up til they're at least 50 these days." I wasn't sure that was true, but it made me feel better to say it.

Marleen always thought of everything that could go wrong. She refused to jump her bike over the ditch in my backyard even though I'd been doing it for six months. I wasn't going to give it up just because my best friend was scared, either; it was too much fun. I'd get going real fast down the hill and there were some bumps and I'd feel like the handlebars were about to pull right out of my hands, but then I'd go soaring over the ditch and when I landed, it was such a feeling of having done something. Marleen even took the long way around to get to my house so she wouldn't have to walk through the black neighborhood. It was only a block and a half away if you went the short way, but Marleen always walked about three blocks out of her way. She said her mom wanted her to, and she probably did. Marleen's mom hated living so close to black people.

"So, did you enjoy talking to my brother this morning?" Marleen knew I liked Kyle, although I tried to act like he irritated me when he pulled my hair or took the television remote away from us when we were at Marleen's.

"Oh honestly!" I rolled my eyes. "I was just glad it wasn't Jeff." We made faces at each other and laughed. I stopped laughing, though, because it made my stomach feel queasy. I folded my arms across my middle and rolled over, facedown on the carpet. The nap of the carpet tickled the inside of my nose and the wanting to hear the telephone ring was heavy in my throat and chest, but at least I didn't feel like I was going to lose my hold on the floor at any second and go soaring up into space.

Marleen was silent. I was sure she wanted to say something, but there was nothing to say, we could only wait. I fought the urge to run to the bathroom and throw up as the silence and time stretched, taffy-like, through the room.

Finally the telephone broke the silence. I jumped up and answered the hall phone and yelled hello before Julie could say anything although I heard her breathing on the extension.

"Hello yourself." Mom laughed at my exuberance. "Would you like to say that a little more quietly to your brother?"

And I collapsed on the floor and realized for the first time how sweet relief really can feel.

## Chapter Three

David always sent Mom the best roses. Perfect roses with perfect blooms and an elegant scent. None of Mom's roses ever nodded their heads too early or faded too fast. They bloomed to perfection then elegantly dropped their petals, revealing their naked golden centers. David always claimed it was Mom who preserved them, Mom always claimed it was David's love that gave the roses beauty.

A perfect rose graces the counter when I arrive. Just one, glorious in its loneliness. I know David didn't give this one to mom. Probably Dougie. He inherited his father's charm, why not this skill, too? I stand in the silent, familiar house for several seconds looking at the rose, letting my consciousness sink deeper and deeper into it, as if into sleep. I imagine myself sliding over the petals into the darkness that guards the golden center. Falling…

I push myself away from the counter and look around, but I can't force myself to take in the whole room. I focus instead on individual objects. The lamp shaped like a lily with a glass shade that my mother has owned since before I was born. The soft quilt made by David's mom. A spot on the carpet I vaguely remember scrubbing fruitlessly. Everything's a little older, a little smaller, a little more worn than the last time I saw it.

No one's home. They're probably at the hospital with David. I decide to take a drive down memory lane.

From my car, Mrs. Whitford's garden looks the same as my memories of it. Unlike our house, I can look at the whole picture here. At this time of the summer in the North Carolina mountains, the roses are at their peak color, although the azaleas are long faded. Tall purple irises nod at me over the dried stems of the daffodils. But the roses, the red and gold, the pink and white and orange, dominate the space inside the white picket fence. Although I don't want to get out of my car, I can remember a time when this tiny garden was the center of my universe.

Someone's home when I return to the house. I don't have to look in the garage to know it. I don't have to hear the thumping music to know who it is. I slam the door on purpose and yell, "Hey Butthead, turn that crap down!"

Dougie comes to the stairs, handsome, young, the image of what his father was. In a couple of minutes he's thundering down to me, wrapping me in a huge bear hug and lifting me off my feet. "Welcome home, Charlie," he roars. "Place hasn't been the same without you. In fact, it's been downright cool."

I gasp and struggle out of his embrace, feigning breathlessness. "You idiot, you nearly knocked me out with that stranglehold." He laughs and we sit down on the couch. The music continues to thump away upstairs, masking the fact that our laughter has already spent itself.

"How's Mom?" I try not to sound too concerned with his answer, although I am. Dougie tries not to sound too glad I asked, although he is.

"She's a little hurt." Dougie holds up a hand when I open my mouth to protest. "She can't figure why you didn't come home when she first called you. Dad's missed you a lot, too."

"I know." The guilt warms me unpleasantly. "I should've come home sooner."

"Mom's afraid you're letting go of the important stuff, losing your values or something." Dougie shrugs. "Now you're getting married and she really wants you to come here to do it. Dad won't be able to make the long trip down there."

"I know." I sigh and sit back on the couch, leaning my head on the cushions and looking at the ceiling. "Growing up sucks, doesn't it?"

Later, I sit in my old room. In front of me, my old paperboard jewelry box sits on my desk. Quite a lot of the white, pink and yellow paper has worn off the box, leaving large gray splotches. I run my fingers over the box. I know what's inside. I'm not sure I want to open it.

I was a happy child, though my father left us when I was two. By the time I turned three, I barely remembered him. My mother was all I needed, and she was one of those unusual selfless people who can suppress their own needs and desires in favor of another's. I didn't understand until I was much older what a void I'd created in her by growing up and needing her less.

Then David came along and I had to come to terms with not being the only center of my mother's universe. Six months after their first date, Mom and David held hands while they told me they were engaged. Five months after the tiny garden wedding, we moved into the big house on the hill that David bought for us. The big house was only two blocks away from where I'd grown up, but it felt like a different world. That night, David asked my permission to adopt me. So I lucked out again and ended up with two parents.

## Chapter Four

The Whitford garden bordered Marleen's back yard. Mr. Whitford planted the garden before I was born. It took up an acre of his land. It had two pine trees, a dozen rose bushes, a low hedge around the exterior border and a fountain in the middle. Mr. Whitford planted daffodils, narcissi, morning glories, peonies and irises. Daisies were not allowed. Daisies were weeds.

Mr. Whitford hated us kids. From the time I could walk independently to Marleen's house, we had an ongoing rivalry. Kyle, Jeff, Marleen and I would sneak up to the barbed wire fence Mr. Whitford had erected two feet away from the white picket fence surrounding his garden. We'd whisper and point, drawn to the garden as if a pied piper were concealed beneath the rose bushes. Mr. Whitford ignored us as long as we didn't touch the fence. The moment a fingertip or toe crossed the line, however, he'd bellow and run at us, waving whatever he had in his hand whether it was a towel or a hoe. We'd run shrieking to the other side of the house, where we'd stay, gasping for breath until one of us--usually Kyle--got the nerve to peek around again.

Nobody ever saw Mrs. Whitford, although the rumor was that Mr. Whitford planted the garden for her. I remember hearing that she had been extraordinarily beautiful in her youth. Every now and then I'd glimpse a white hand with plump blue veins gracefully crisscrossing the prominent bones as it pulled the curtain at the back of the Whitford house. Once I even thought I saw a round white face with sunken black eyes, almost skull-like. But Mrs. Whitford remained a mystery to all of us, not that we'd have it any other way. In fact, when Mr. Whitford passed away the summer I turned ten, and my mother and Mrs. Galloway went to visit Mrs. Whitford to offer help and whatever solace they could, I stayed away.

The barbed wire fence came down and a neat picket fence went up when Mrs. Whitford's son Brian arrived to take care of her. The garden grew wild that summer, but when Mrs. Whitford passed away a year later, we started to see Brian working in the garden. He didn't mind us watching him, and he sometimes came over to talk to us. Marleen started spending a lot of time outside. When I went home with her after school, which I did more and more often after Mom had the baby, Marleen always suggested having a soda on her old swingset or sitting on her deck. Once when I got there late, I saw her talking to Brian. They were laughing, and Brian put up a hand and pushed his hair back from his eyes. His hand looked really small and white outlined against his dark hair.

"He's an artist," Marleen said. "And he doesn't mind us coming into the garden." She led me down one of the garden paths, and I ducked out of the way of rose bush branches snapping back into my face. She paused and placed her hand beneath a late rose, which was just beginning to lose its bloom. "I bet Brian likes to paint the roses," she said, a dreamy look on her face.

I wasn't certain I liked the reality of being in the garden. From outside, it was a place of mystery and beauty. An enchanted garden from a fairytale held no more intrigue than the Whitford garden when viewed from outside the picket fence. But now that I was inside, I found that the paths were overgrown, rosebush thorns tore my skin and insects of every type buzzed about at unexpected times. Something small and black scuttled from under one bush to under another one.

But then we came to a little clearing with a few large rocks, presumably too large for Mr. Whitford to move when he first made the garden. Instead of moving them, he'd placed a birdbath between them. Marleen sat down on one of the rocks and I sat down on another. I faced Marleen's house, which suited me fine, especially when, a moment later, Kyle's Camaro pulled up. I sat up a little straighter, completely missing whatever Marleen was saying about something funny that had happened to her in gym class.

Kyle wasn't alone. The passenger door of the Camaro popped open and a girl with long red hair got out. Her hair shone like a red gold setting sun as it fanned about her and fell gracefully past her hips. Kyle bent closer to her and I heard her laugh as she pushed him away and ran up the walk toward the house. Kyle didn't even look our way as he followed her.

"Who's that?" I interrupted Marleen's oration about Jim Reese's pants being pulled down in the middle of a volleyball game.

"You know Jim Reese. Fat kid with the lazy eye…"

"No, the redhead." I gestured toward Marleen's house.

"Oh, her. Tracy Collins. She just moved here. Kyle's been showing her around, if you know what I mean." Marleen made kissing sounds into the air and rolled her eyes.

I felt fairly certain I knew exactly what she meant. Jealousy is an ugly and very uncomfortable feeling, but I almost welcomed the twinge I received at Marleen's words.

"Charlie, are you listening to me at all?" Marleen frowned in my direction. I looked up but didn't answer. A bee buzzed out of the rosebushes and landed in her hair. Marleen immediately jumped up and ran shrieking out of the garden, waving her hands wildly. I followed her out, but when she invited me to come inside, I decided I'd better head home. Mom would want me home soon. She and the baby weren't sleeping in the afternoon anymore.

David always left work about six, so Mom planned dinner for six fifteen. I was supposed to have all my homework done by the time he arrived so we could relax and eat dinner and catch up on our days together. I was later than usual and I knew the algebra homework in my backpack would be hard enough to keep me busy for at least an hour, so I hurried to put away my bike and go inside.

The house was dim in the gathering dusk, but a soft sound emanated from the hallway. I approached with caution. The baby sitting outside the hall bathroom turned his head and fixed me with a stare. "Mom, your baby's in the hall!" I yelled. He'd just learned to roll over and scoot (a little early for a baby, Mom said) and Mom had been talking about baby gates and plugs for the electrical outlets for several weeks. She hadn't done anything yet, though.

"He's fine! I'll be out in a minute!" Mom yelled back from the bathroom. I looked back at the baby. He stuck his finger in his mouth and drooled as he stared back at me.

The bathroom door opened and Mom came out. She looked from the baby to me to the small puddle of drool on the floor. I made a disgusted face. "Why's he drool so much?"

"He's teething." Mom scooped up the baby, ignoring the drool. "I'm fixing pork chops for dinner, you want to help?"

I loved helping Mom in the kitchen. She was an excellent cook, and I learned a lot from her. But not today. Today she'd want to know how my day was and if anything interesting happened. She might even be able to get something out of me about Kyle's new girlfriend. Mom didn't know about my crush on Kyle and I preferred to keep it that way. "I've got homework." I shook my backpack. When I saw the disappointment on her face, though, I said quickly, "I'll help you with the cleanup, though, okay?"

"Sure." She smiled and patted my cheek. "Go get that homework done."

After dinner, Mom washed the dishes and I dried. Before the baby, I loved washing dishes with Mom because we would talk without anybody else around, even David. Now Mom was too tired to talk. I stared at the soapy water as Mom put a dish under the faucet. The soapsuds rinsed down the drain, leaving her red chapped hands and the smooth clean china.

"Penny for your thoughts." Mom's voice surprised me.

I jumped. I'd been thinking about Tracy, imagining her and Kyle cruising the town in his Camaro. Had they been parking yet? Had Kyle made it to second base? Further? I found myself wishing a horrible fate on Tracy. But I didn't even know her, so with the jealousy came guilt. And I couldn't tell my mother any of this.

"I was thinking about an algebra problem on my homework," I said. "I don't think I answered it right."

Mom sighed and let the water out. David looked up from his seat in the living room. He was giving the baby a bottle. Mom hadn't been able to breastfeed this time. Her milk never came in. She said she didn't mind having a bottle baby, but sometimes she looked sort of lost when David was feeding the baby while she sat with empty arms. Now, Mom folded the dishcloth and laid it neatly over the faucet to dry. “Then you should probably go check it.”

As I headed for the door, she called me back. “If you need help, I’m here.”

I nodded, waved and sprinted up the steps.

## Chapter Five

On Friday, I spent the night at Marleen's. Mom didn't really like for me to spend the night away from home, so this was a rare treat. "Have her over here," Mom would always say, never seeming to realize how difficult that was. Mom liked Marleen because Marleen always behaved well in front of parents. "She's quiet and ladylike," Mom said. "Maybe some of it will rub off on you." To which I'd reply that if Mom didn't want a tomboy for a daughter, she shouldn't have let my real dad give me a boy's name.

But even Mom had to admit that if I kept turning Marleen's invitations around and insisting she sleep over at my house, somebody would get offended. Marleen didn't mind, but her mother was sort of touchy. Mom said Mrs. Galloway came from the wrong side of the tracks and often thought other people didn't think she was good enough for them. Besides, I wanted an opportunity to see Kyle up close without seeming too obvious. And Friday should be perfect since Marleen's parents were going out and leaving Kyle in charge.

"I hope Jeff doesn't bug us too much," Marleen said. Her brother Jeff had become a little creepy, in a greasemonkey kind of way. "God, I wish I just had one adorable brother like you do. You know Kyle's planning to bring his new girlfriend over?"

I shrugged, as if I didn't care. She knew, of course, but I hated to admit my hopeless crush, even to my best friend.

But Marleen just sighed. "Neither of them has an artistic soul, you know? I mean, all Jeff cares about is cars and all Kyle cares about is girls. There's so much more to life than that. No one understands me. Well, no one but…"

She broke off, but I suspected I knew who she was talking about. She'd been over to Mrs. Whitford's garden again, talking to Brian. I didn't go with her when Brian was in the garden anymore. I wasn't sure why, but it seemed weird to me that he was so interested in talking to Marleen when he was a good twenty years old than her.

Brian wasn't in the garden when we got to Marleen's house, and Kyle wasn't home yet, so I let Marleen convince me to go to the garden. Most of the roses had withered, and there weren't so many bugs as during the summer, but the garden still had a creepy feel to it. Marleen and I discussed the school Halloween dance for a while. Who was taking who. Who wasn't going. Who would probably kiss who. Who would ask us to dance if we decided it was worth our while to go.

The back screen door at the house banged shut and we peered through the thinning bushes to see Brian pulling spades and hoes and shovels out of the storage area in the basement of the old house. He didn't appear to have seen us, and with difficulty I managed to hold Marleen down. I didn't want to have to talk to him. She giggled but acquiesced.

We watched as Brian pulled what seemed like every gardening tool he owned out of the storage closet, then seemed to find what he was looking for. He stood, stretched, and turned slowly, his eyes scanning the garden, a trowel in one hand, a bag of bulbs in the other. As we crouched in the garden, the scent of damp earth and rotting plants filling our nostrils, Brian drove the trowel into the ground again and again. I could hear the thud of its blade, the ripping sounds of roots and sometimes a tiny clink as it hit a rock or pebble.

Finally, tired of watching Brian thrusting into the earth, I tugged on Marleen's shirttail. She shook her head and stayed where she was. I shrugged and headed for the fence, crawling with my head down. I wasn't able to see Brian or tell for sure if he saw me, but the stabbing noises continued. Only later, when Marleen joined me in her yard did I realize that Brian couldn't have escaped seeing us from his back porch as he came outside. Somehow realizing he'd known we were there and acted like he hadn't creeped me out even more.

Kyle did bring Tracy over. I found it harder to hate her than I'd anticipated. She had a wonderful laugh that just made everyone around her want to laugh, too, and she spent a lot of time talking to Marleen and me, more time than she spent hanging all over Kyle, in fact. She told me what color eye shadow to use to bring out the tiny gold and green flecks in what

I had always considered my plain brown eyes. She told Marleen she could trim her hair so it would flip back in the latest style. She admired my earrings and bemoaned the fact that her parents wouldn't let her have pierced ears.

For dinner, Kyle ordered a pizza, and we all gathered in the kitchen to eat it. Marleen and I sat at the table, our eyes on Kyle, who perched on the kitchen counter munching on pizza, and Tracy, who bustled about the kitchen filling everyone's glasses with soda and making sure we all had enough pizza. When Kyle began teasing Marleen about some movie star she'd had a crush on months before, Tracy reached up and smacked him on the side of the head. "Leave your sister alone," she ordered. "Eat your pizza."

"Yes, ma'am," Kyle said, pretending to be meek, then seizing her around the waist and tickling her. When I saw the way he looked at her, green fingers of envy crawled over me, but my resentment uncomfortably mixed with admiration for her. I liked her, I wanted to be like her--I wished a lightning bolt would come down from the heavens, strike her down and leave Kyle for me.

Jeff walked in. He raised his eyebrows as Kyle released Tracy. "Don't let me interrupt." He snagged a piece of pizza and swaggered back outside.

The door snapped shut behind him just as Tracy, a smile on her face, opened her mouth to offer Jeff a soda. "Ignore him."

Kyle rubbed her shoulders. Did he ever stop touching her? "My little brother's a tad on the wacky side. Everybody says it."

"He seems lonely." Tracy looked out the window to where Jeff had disappeared behind the metal building he kept his tools and car stuff in. Antifreeze and oil. Spare parts. Old tires. An old crumbling stone wall separated the driveway from the yard. Jeff sat back there a lot when he wasn't messing around inside the building.

"He's probably smoking something," Marleen said.

"Marleen!" Kyle gaped at her. Then he laughed. "Sometimes you surprise me, lil sis." When Tracy turned to him with her eyebrows raised, he shrugged. "Well, she's probably right."

I didn't know if Marleen was right or not. I wasn't even certain I cared if Jeff was smoking something, illegal or not. But when Kyle looked at Tracy like she was the only person in the room, I felt just as lonely as Tracy imagined Jeff was.

"I'm so glad I've got one normal brother," Marleen sighed, looking up at the ceiling of her basement.

One of the things I loved about spending the night with Marleen was the finished basement that her family used as a den. Half of the room was a wet bar/kitchenette, and there were always plenty of snacks for overnight visits and midnight raids.

The other half had a television and VCR, couch and easy chair. And there was plenty of space, if we scooted the coffee table to the side, for two sleeping bags. We imagined ourselves completely private when we slept in the basement.

I rolled over in my sleeping bag. It was dark in Marleen's basement, except for a light on the microwave and a bit of illumination coming from the rectangular windows high above us. I propped myself up on my elbows, feeling the scratchy shag carpeting under my elbows. I had no difficulty imagining the carpet as moss on the floor of an underground tomb.

"Do you think he loves her?" The question seemed all important and totally logical to my mind.

Marleen snorted. "Oh geez, Charlie, you're so stuck on my brother, aren't you?" I blushed, but in the dark she couldn't tell. She continued, "Maybe he thinks he's in love with her, but I doubt he actually loves her, you know?"

I did know, and the observation surprised me. Marleen wasn't the smartest person in our class. I always thought I was more intelligent than her, as a matter of fact. But her distinction between "in love" and "love" made sense. Loving someone involved the kind of devotion my mother had for my brother and me. She'd do anything for us, just like I would for her. Being "in love" was more of a selfish thing, kind of like what I felt for Kyle. When you were "in love", you were in it for your own pleasure, not so much for the other person.

I've always credited Marleen with leading me to the first adult realization of my life. And I've never forgotten her, for that very reason.

## Chapter Six

Love or in love, it didn't really matter much over the next few weeks. Kyle and Tracy were inseparable. They were Homecoming King and Queen. They attended the parties with the other cool couples and made out behind the high school gym between classes--or so I heard. Gossip was pretty bloated by the time it drifted down to the junior high school, and even I realized that. There was no denying, however, that Kyle and Tracy were the town's teen golden couple.

Lucky me, I got to see them on a regular basis, too. After school, Marleen was unwilling to do much more than sit in Mrs. Whitford's garden discussing art and the immaturity of the boys in our class. Sometimes when Brian came out, she'd wave and smile brightly. But when she wanted to go talk to him, I always decided it was time to leave.

"There's Brian, let's go talk to him," she said.

"Why?" Every time I asked I hoped maybe she could explain it to me.

"He's lonely. He's got to be. I mean, he's all alone in that big house. I never see any friends there with him."

"Maybe there's a reason for that." I looked with distaste at Brian's soiled white shirt. "He's so dirty."

But Marleen imagined Brian's wiry muscles beneath his shirt. I could see it in her eyes. And she excused his filthy appearance easily. “He’s an artist, Charlie. That’s paint on his shirt.”

“And under his fingernails and around his neck.” I stood. “Yeah. You go ahead, Marleen. I gotta get home.”

Marleen didn’t need any further urging. Without a backward glance, she walked directly over to Brian. But as I turned to head in the opposite direction, I felt a twinge of misgiving and glanced over my shoulder. Though I wasn’t sure why, I felt Marleen should be more careful with Brian, especially when I saw him immediately put down the bag of fertilizer he was carrying and walk to the fence to talk to her.

My bike leaned against Jeff’s metal building, but I didn’t know he was there until I smelled the smoke. I froze, looking guilty, almost as if I were the one who’d been caught smoking. He looked back at me, removed the white stick from his mouth and blew a smoke ring. “Wanna smoke?”

“No.”

“Didn’t think so.” He turned away from me.

I hesitated for a moment, looking curiously at the cylinder and thinking about Marleen’s remark that Jeff was smoking “something”. Curiosity got the best of me. “What is it?”

His mouth quirked. “Just a little weed.” I must have gasped because he laughed a little. “Cigarette, idiot. You want some or not?”

“No,” I said, but I sat down on the wall next to him. The weeds had died back a little, but the spot still felt secluded. I wasn't sure why I was sitting there with Marleen's greasemonkey brother, but I was uncertain about leaving until I knew Marleen had returned from her chat with Brian. And it felt rude to sit somewhere else when I knew Jeff was already sitting here.

Jeff made no comment, but continued to smoke his cigarette and blow smoke rings. I admired his ability in spite of myself. "You're good at that."

"Lots of practice."

"Why do you sit back here all the time?" I looked at the rusted back of the metal building. I couldn't imagine the draw.

Jeff shrugged and took a long draw off his cigarette before answering. "Because nobody else likes to sit back here."

"Because of the weeds and bugs."

"Yeah."

"You like weeds and bugs?"

"No."

"So why sit back here with them?"

"I don't like people either." Jeff glared at me.

I nodded. "That makes sense. If you don't like people, the only place to go is where there aren't any. The only place you can be sure there won't be any people is where people don't like to be."

"You talk a lot," Jeff said. Our eyes met and I realized for the first time that he had very nice eyes. Blue green with flecks of gold. They reminded me of a description I'd read once about the Mediterranean Sea.

"Geez, Charlie, you won't talk to my neighbor, but you'll come smoke with my weirdo brother." Marleen's voice rose, accusatory and ridiculing, from behind us.

I jumped up, feeling and looking guilty. "I wanted to make sure you made it back okay."

Marleen snickered. "I'm fine. What was Brian going to do? Carry me off?"

"Who knows?" Her laughter stung, especially on top of my own guilt. "Maybe. Mr. Whitford might have done that!"

Marleen rolled her eyes. "You're so immature, Charlie. Stay here with my brother. You guys should be on exactly the same level."

She marched away, and I looked down at Jeff for some sign of sympathy. Without looking at me, he smashed out his cigarette, jumped down into the weeds and walked away.

Marleen's attitude toward me over the next few weeks stung. She snubbed me at school, stopped inviting me over and didn't return my calls. After two weeks of this, I rode my bike over, ready to brave Brian Whitford if necessary. Jeff was in the driveway, lying on top of the hood of Kyle's Camaro.

I pulled up next to him. I could see the Whitford house and garden, but nobody appeared to be in it. Jeff spat smoke rings at the gray November sky. He wore a tank top and hooded sweatshirt zipped half way up.

"Marleen here?" I tried to sound casual.

Jeff shrugged. "What do you care?" It didn't sound like an insult, just like he was curious and wanted to know.

I opened my mouth, then shut it. What did I care? I'd just been worried about my friend. After all, if anybody had been insulted, it had been me. "I don't." I knew I did.

The screen door slammed, and Kyle came down the steps two at a time, jingling his keys. "Hey Charlie." He nodded at me and turned to his brother. "Get off."

Jeff tossed his cigarette on the ground, slid off the hood of the Camaro and ground the butt into the dust. I noticed a tiny sprig of green clover under the gravel he stirred up. It must have escaped the November frosts somehow.

## Chapter Seven

The loss of Marleen turned out to be sort of a blessing, if I looked on the bright side, anyway. I no longer had to witness Kyle and Tracy's love in first person since I didn't hang out at her house very often. Every now and then I'd see them pass by when I was uptown at the library or going to the store for Mom. I'd be pedaling along balancing a gallon of milk in the basket of my bike when they'd pass and I'd turn to wave, nearly losing my balance.

I wondered often why I wanted to be acknowledged by them, as if they were real royalty, not just Homecoming king and queen in a ratty little town. It bothered me a little, but I couldn't seem to help myself, though at times I thought I hated them both.

Mom was happy I was spending more time at home, anyway. Now that the baby was sleeping more at night, she had loads more energy and she'd started remodeling. I would come home to find her on a stepladder, stripping wallpaper in the hallway or painting stencils in the kitchen while the baby played in the living room. As soon as I walked in, she'd say, "The baby's in the living room, could you watch him while I finish this?" So I'd take my homework into the living room and work on it there while the baby crawled about exploring the thick pile of the beige carpet.

On the Friday after Thanksgiving, I watched him while I studied for a Social Studies test. Just as I finished reading a passage about Benjamin Franklin's newspaper, I looked up to see the baby pick something up from the floor.

"No!" I yelled, jumping up and letting the book slide off my lap onto the floor. "Don't eat that!"

"What is it?" Mom cried, rounding the corner from the hallway at a run.

"He ate something off the floor!" I cried, distressed and picturing myself doing the Heimlich maneuver on his tiny frame.

"Oh." Mom looked relieved. "Don't worry, Hon. It was probably just a Cheerio." She headed into the kitchen. "Your dad's going to be late. You want some leftover turkey and dressing for dinner?"

I walked to the door to the kitchen so I could watch her. Mom often called David my "dad", and I usually didn't mind. For some reason, that afternoon her casual reference to my dad brought up an uncomfortable memory. It was during the summer, an afternoon when I went swimming with Marleen. Mom was supposed to pick me up after the baby's well child checkup. When she didn't show up, I walked to David's office.

"Charlie," he said in surprise when his secretary called him out of a closing to find me dripping in the reception area of his real estate office. "What happened?" He was quick to console me, found me a blanket, assured me that Mom would be horrified when she realized what she'd done, although that didn't seem likely since she evidently hadn't gone straight home from the doctor's office. "She probably had some shopping to do and forgot she had someplace else to be, sweetie," he assured me. "Wait here while I finish this up, then I'll take you home."

Mom was horrified, just as David had said she'd be. He chided her gently about it, and she hugged me and apologized. I couldn't deny that I'd been hurt. My mother had never forgotten me before.

"Why do you call him that?" I asked now.

"Hmmm?" Mom surveyed the refrigerated remains of our Thanksgiving dinner.

"David. Why do you call him my dad?" I wasn't sure why I asked the question. Surely David was my father in every real sense. Still, it seemed a little cold to completely ignore the man who made it biologically possible for me to exist.

Mom turned with a foil-wrapped package of turkey in her hands. Her face looked frozen, like somebody had doused her with cold water.

"Why would you ask me something like that?" Her voice sounded flat, almost toneless, the kind of voice a dead woman might use.

I shrugged. "Sorry. I didn't mean to say something wrong. It's just--you talk about David all the time like he's my father. He's Dougie's father, but he's not really mine."

"How can you say that?" Now Mom looked hurt. She slapped the foil package onto the cutting board. "Have you forgotten all that David's done for you? What's the matter with you?"

"I'm not being ungrateful, Mom." I couldn't seem to stop myself. "It's just a fact. David's not my father. I don't even know who my father is."

"Did it ever occur to you that you might be better off?" Mom's hands were trembling. She placed them carefully on the counter.

The question stopped me in mid-thought. Better off? Could I be better off not knowing the answer to the questions I'd thought of off and on for years? Who was my father? Why did he leave? How was it better not to know?

Mom fiddled with the tin foil, pulling back a corner and putting it back, as if she felt if she unwrapped it totally, she'd never be able to contain it again. She took a deep breath and looked up at me. "You should know, your 'real father,' as you call him, gave you up."

"What?" I jerked my eyes back to her face, distracted from the aluminum foil.

"He gave you up. I wrote to him when David and I decided to get married. I asked him to give up his parental rights so David could adopt you. And he did. No questions asked. That's why you're better off. David is your father."

The full implication of what she'd said hit me a second after she'd finished speaking. "You mean you knew how to get in touch with him? You had to write him, you had to contact him to get him to give up his parental rights? How come you never told *me* how to write to him?"

Mom gave me a startled look and refolded the corner of foil over the turkey. "I--"

"You didn't tell me he'd have to give up his parental rights when you asked me if David could adopt me." I was angrier with my mother than I'd ever been before. It was sort of startling to go from peace to rage like that. "You didn't ask me if that was okay."

"Charlie, we thought …" Her voice trailed off, and I knew she couldn't come up with an excuse. She knew what they had done had been wrong.

I shook my head. "You thought I was too young to make a decision like that, didn't you? You treat me like a kid, Mom! How about all those times I asked about my father? Did you know how to get in touch with him all those times?"

Mom reached out to touch my arm. I jumped back. "Don't touch me!" I shouted. "You stole him from me, but you did that a long time ago, didn't you? He's part of who I am, Mom, and even you can't deny that!"

My screaming frightened the baby and he started crying. When my mother glanced toward the living room, I bolted upstairs and slammed my door. I listened and a moment later I heard my mother's footsteps outside. She paused outside my door, then continued on to the baby's room.

## Chapter Eight

A tense atmosphere settled over our house after my fight with mom. When David got home from work, I heard them talking, but the regular rise and fall of their voices had been disrupted. Mom's voice sounded higher, shriller than usual and David's was much lower. Slowly his lower voice formed a velvety pit for Mom's voice to fall into, his words gently rocking her, soothing. I was sorry for what I'd done to David, but I couldn't apologize to Mom. Betrayal stung too fresh, and every time I thought of her lie of omission, I got angry all over again.

When the voices stopped, David came and knocked on my door. I pretended to be asleep. I didn't want to talk to him, but mostly I didn't want to see the hurt look on his face. I felt like he and I were both victims of Mom's betrayal.

David cornered me the next morning. I thought I was safe, coming down around nine o'clock, but he hadn't gone to work like he usually did on Saturday mornings. I felt guilty when I saw him. David worked hard, and he was dedicated to his job. I knew he'd stayed home because of me. He sat in the family room reading a newspaper when I came in with my cereal. Mom and the baby were nowhere to be seen.

David folded his paper. "We need to talk."

"Crap." I bit my lip and clenched my hand into a fist. "Mom went and complained to you, right? She's the one--"

"Your mother did what she felt she had to do." David gave me a stern look. "You don't know your father, it's true. But the reason you don't know him is that he wasn't a very nice man. He wasn't a father like your friends have, Charlie."

I thought of the other fathers I knew. Marleen's dad, who worked at the quarry and went drinking with his buddies afterward. I'd never been around him much, but when I was, the stench of his breath always made me uncomfortable. Other dads weren't much better. The most popular girl in my class, Stephanie Clark, for instance. Her dad was a lawyer and they lived in the rich section of town in a big white house. But her dad was always going on long business trips and taking his secretary with him.

In fact, when I thought about it, a lot of my friends envied me my stepfather. Especially Marleen. She'd told me many times how lucky I was. I couldn't blame Marleen. Her father reminded me of a gorilla. His arms were too long, knotted with muscles, and he always wore his sleeveless tank top undershirt with wiry hair poking out of the top and the armholes.

I loved David, but something in me yearned to know where I'd come from. I wondered what my real father was like, why my mother was so determined to protect me from him that she'd break our trust. Curiosity killed the cat. Maybe he'd been someone awful, a thief or a drunk or maybe, and the very thought filled me with horror, maybe he'd been a wife-beater. Had he beaten my mother? Or me, when I was too young to remember? Had I been wrong to condemn my mother?

David took my hand and when I looked at him he smiled. "I know it's hard, baby." I was startled to see the tears in his eyes. "But you can't let something like this come between you and your mom."

I nodded, my throat tight. "I'm sorry, David. You're a great dad. I don't mean to be ungrateful." Or at least, I wanted to say that, but he pulled me into a hug before I could finish. I think he knew, though.

I apologized to my mom, too. I never quite met her eyes when I did it, and maybe she felt like I wasn't as sincere as I should've been, but she accepted my apology a little stiffly. Later, as I was studying for an algebra test, she came into my room and touched my shoulder. She held a piece of paper in her hands, an uncertain expression on her face.

"Hey." She fingered the paper, running it through her fingers, a nervous motion that was out of character for her.

"Hey," I said. "You'll get a paper cut if you keep doing that."

She laughed, but the laugh was all in her mouth and it ended quickly. "This is for you." She put the paper down in front of me.

I recognized my mother's loopy, elegant handwriting, but something held me back from reading what was written there. "What is it?"

"It's your father's address."

I went for a bike ride. I tried not to think about the reality of the slip of paper I'd left on my desk at home. I'd wondered about my father for so long it had become like an obsession, growing in the dark places of my mind, pale and lumpy like mushrooms. Now I had the power to find out something about my father, I wasn't sure what to do with myself.

Mom hadn't helped, either. When I asked her what she wanted me to do with the address, she said only, "David and I think you're old enough to make that decision yourself. We trust you."

So I was on my own.

Late fall in the North Carolina mountains is a deceptive time. Some days the sky is clear and blue and looks like summer. Other days it hangs gray and low, like fog that hasn't reached the ground yet. But most deceptive of all are the trees. Deprived of their leaves, they stretch their long limbs to the heavens, and when you look at all of them together, they appear almost soft, like if you fell from the sky, you'd bounce off the sharp points rather than being impaled. The trees fool you that way.

Just two streets over from us, four streets from Marleen's, the upper class lived. Lawns weren't just cut, they were manicured. Maids and gardeners and even cooks came and went from these houses. I used to wish I lived there. Instead I just rode my bike there.

The cool air felt good on my face on that late fall day. I stood up and pedaled hard, pushing the bike, feeling the strain on my muscles as I propelled myself uphill, then settled down and coasted downhill. Using the momentum I'd built up, I glided around the corner and down Oak Hill Street. Friction won out over gravity and I began slowly pedaling again, looking at the large houses. David had just sold one over here. I wondered which one.

Outside a large house with huge white columns, a girl played with a small brown and white spotted dog. In the autumn sunlight, her hair glowed like fire, like the leaves that had recently fallen from the maple trees. As I passed, she raised her hand and smiled. "Charlie, hey!"

Almost involuntarily, I braked. I watched as Tracy wrestled a small ball from the dog, then tossed it toward the house and walked over to me. "How are you?" She laughed when the dog came bounding back to her, the ball clenched in his mouth.

"Fine." I couldn't believe I was standing outside the house of my arch nemesis having a calm chat. Would we talk about the weather, too?

"I haven't seen you in a while. Down, Petey." The dog stopped jumping at her and settled down with the ball between his front paws. "How come you don't hang out with Marleen anymore?"

How could I explain it? "We had a fight," was the best I could come up with.

"Well, sure, but you guys have been friends for a long time, right? You can't let one fight ruin a friendship like that." She looked sad. "Believe me, real friends are hard to come by. If I didn't have Kyle, I don't know what I'd do."

"You and Kyle are friends?" I realized how dumb the question sounded as soon as I asked it.

But Tracy didn't seem to think it was a dumb question. "Of course. We're more than friends, too, but we're definitely friends. Kyle's the only real friend I've been able to make since I moved here." She touched my shoulder. "You should talk to Marleen. She's been lonely, I know."

"How do you know?" I found it surprisingly easy to imagine Tracy and Marleen having a heart to heart discussion. They'd braid each others' hair as they talked, a braid of sandy brown and one of red-gold. Perhaps Marleen would cry a little, her tear falling on Tracy's braid, turning the red-gold into auburn.

"She told me," Tracy said. "She misses you. She needs a friend. Call her."

I nodded. "Maybe I will."

"Do it. You won't regret it." She looked up at the sky. "It almost looks like snow, doesn't it?"

"Yeah, I gotta go, Tracy." I put one foot on a pedal and balanced the bike.

"Sure," she stepped back. "But call Marleen, okay, Charlie? She really does miss you." She smiled suddenly. "Hey, wasn't it your dad who sold us this house? My parents are still talking about how great he was."

"Yeah, he is great," I agreed. "Bye, Tracy."

She waved at me from the end of her driveway. I rounded the corner and looked back to see her playing catch with Petey again.

I called Marleen. She invited me over and I met her at her house. Awkward as it was, I put my Dad's address in an envelope without looking at it and took it with me. Marleen handled it with suitable reverence. "So what are you going to do?" We sat outside her house in sight of the Whitford house, but we hadn't gone into Mrs. Whitford's garden. It was cold.

"I don't know," I shifted in the lawn chair Marleen had brought out for me. It looked wrong on the November lawn, as if it shouldn't be used except when the grass was emerald green and the temperature had risen above eighty degrees. The lawn chair belonged to another world from the one we were sitting in.

"Well, you don't really have to do anything, do you?" Marleen raised her eyebrows and handed the envelope back to me.

I was surprised. Marleen had listened with sympathy to my worries about who my father was. I hadn't expected this response from her. "What do you mean?"

"I mean, the point was to be trusted with the information, right? So, your mom trusted you. I mean, seriously, Charlie, you don't really think this guy is going to replace David in your life, do you? Do you want to replace David?"

"Of course not!" I snapped. "It's just that now that I could find out something, maybe I should. You know, it's like I have this algebra equation to solve but I never knew what the letters stood for. Now I do, and all that's left is sitting down to solve it."

"Maybe it shouldn't be solved." Marleen shrugged. "This isn't a test."

I shook my head. "You just don't understand, Marleen." Although I couldn't put my feelings into words, I thought that in my heart I wanted to touch the hand of the man who'd sown the seed that had grown into me. I'd never have said that out loud though.

Marleen smiled a little. "Maybe I understand better than you think. I mean, you haven't even read it, have you? You don't know what his name is. You're afraid if you look at it, you'll have to keep going. You'll have to track him down."

I had to admit she was probably right. I looked down at the envelope in my hands. Marleen suddenly reached out and covered my hands with one of hers. "Fine, but just don't read it until you are absolutely positively certain you want to know about him. Because once you know, you can't go back."

I put the slip of paper into my jewelry box. It was an old one made of painted paperboard with a little plastic ballerina inside who pirouetted in front of a mirror when I lifted the lid. I wasn't certain what to do about my father, so I decided to do nothing for now. Maybe Marleen was right. Maybe having the power to do something was all that I required. Before I closed the lid, I put the couple of bits of jewelry I owned into the box on top of the envelope. A charm bracelet, a couple of pins I'd claimed from Mom's jewelry box, a plastic ring I got out of a gumball machine once. They looked odd on top of the white paper envelope.

When I kissed Mom and David goodnight, there was a little strain, mostly, I sensed, because they'd like to have asked me what I was going to do. Perhaps they wished they could still offer me some guidance. I gave David an extra hug, kissed the baby, who blinked his wide blue eyes at me, then started up the stairs.

The phone rang. I heard Mom answer it, give a soft exclamation a moment later, then call me. “Charlie, come here for a minute.”

I turned and came back, curious. “What’s up?”

“Mrs. Collins is on the line, sweetie. She wondered if you knew where Tracy is.”

“Why would I know--?” I remembered. “Oh, I did see her this afternoon in her yard. She was playing with their dog. Have they checked with Kyle?”

But Mom was busy relaying the information to Mrs. Collins. After a moment, she hung up. She stood still for a minute, then wrapped her arms around herself and turned to me. “Tracy disappeared this afternoon. She was supposed to meet Kyle at the movies, but she never showed. Edna happened to see Charlie talking to her outside. But Tracy never came inside afterward. Edna thought Kyle had stopped by and they’d gone on to the movies, although she said it was strange Tracy didn’t bring the dog in.”

“Disappeared?” The word made me nervous. How many times was it used in the course of a normal day? My keys have disappeared. Can you find the dog? He seems to have disappeared. I can’t imagine where my money keeps disappearing. But when it referred to a person, especially one I knew, I felt its chilling roots take hold of my heart and squeeze.

Mom shook her head as if to clear it. “It’s probably nothing, Hon. Maybe she’d had a fight with her parents or Kyle and just wants to make them worry.”

“No way. Tracy’s not like that. She wouldn’t do something like this just to get attention.”

David came into the kitchen. “Then maybe there’s some other explanation.”

I looked at him hopefully, but when I saw Mom doing the same thing, I shivered a little. David put his arms around both of us. “I’m sure everything is fine,” he said, but for some reason, all I could think of was how the flowers in Mrs. Whitford’s garden were pretty and bright, but dark things scuttled underneath.

## Chapter Nine

I'm not certain what frightened me most about Tracy's disappearance. I didn't want to think about the bad things that might have happened to her--or that I might have been the last one to see her. In my memory about that afternoon, she appeared transparent, even as she tossed the ball to her solid dog. It was like she was a ghost, the real Tracy was already gone.

But more than my fears for Tracy, I soon came to hate what her disappearance symbolized. My mother had always been willing to let me have a little freedom, at least as far back as I could remember. She didn't have to be looking over my shoulder every minute, or holding my hand every time I went outside. But the next morning as I left for school, she asked me, "Are you coming straight home after school?"

I blinked. Mom hadn't asked me that since fifth grade. "I might go home with Marleen."

"Why don't you bring her here?" Mom looked anxious. "With everything that's going on, I'd just feel better."

"Mom, really." I resisted the urge to roll my eyes. "I'll be fine. How about if I call you if I decide to go to Marleen's?"

Mom hesitated for just a second, then she shook her head and smiled. "Okay. I'm sorry, Hon. I'm just worried. Maybe they've found Tracy by now, anyway. Probably they have."

But they hadn't. Tracy was all anyone talked about at school. I had plenty of time to listen because Marleen didn't show up. I wondered if she'd stayed home because Kyle was so upset over his girlfriend's disappearance. It didn't seem likely, but who knew?

After school, I rode my bike over to Marleen's house. I intended to march right up to her door, knock and find out why she hadn't been in school. However, as I rounded the corner to her house, I skidded to a stop. Three police cars were parked outside. Two policemen stood outside the front door and two more were poking around in the yard. One of them was even pushing aside the weeds behind Jeff's little metal building. Looking for clues? I realized with a shock that the police probably thought Kyle had something to do with Tracy's disappearance. Wasn't it usually the boyfriend?

I rode my bike home, thinking of this new turn of events. Mom sipped tea at the kitchen table, obviously waiting for me. Mom was never just sitting in the kitchen when I got home.

"Hey," she said. "Did you see Marleen?"

"No, she wasn't in school today." I took an apple out of the fruit bowl. "I went by her house."

"Is she okay?" Mom sounded concerned. I knew she cared about Marleen. After all, she'd fed us both afternoon snacks and taken us out for pizza and movies and hosted sleepovers for us most of our lives. "I mean, were she and Tracy that close? I know her brother was dating Tracy."

"I dunno," I chewed my apple. "The police were there."

Mom dropped her teacup and it hit the counter with a loud ringing sound. "The police?"

"Yeah, I mean, Kyle was dating Tracy, right? She was supposed to be meeting him." It sounded like I was trying to make excuses. I knew I was. Police don't poke around in the weeds outside your home unless they're looking for something and feel pretty sure they'll find it.

"Of course." Mom picked up the mug, but I noticed her hands were shaking. "Of course, that must be it. I'm sure they just wanted to ask him some questions about where he was going to meet Tracy."

But Mom's reaction had already confirmed my fears. Having the police at your house the day after your girlfriend disappeared wasn't a good thing and probably indicated you were a suspect.

Of course, later that afternoon, when the police questioned me about the last time I saw Tracy, I felt a little different.

The next day, all I heard was gossip about Kyle and Tracy. I was accosted in the hallway and at lunch by several people wanting to know more about the most exciting thing ever to happen in our tiny town. Gossip had already spread that I was the last to see Tracy and I had been questioned by the cops.

Gossip had also adorned the truth, however, adding that I had actually seen Tracy be kidnapped, had even narrowly escaped the same fate myself.

None of the rumors were true, of course, but they still gave me chills. I tried not to think about Tracy's kidnapper lurking nearby while I talked to her. If there was a kidnapper, of course.

Marleen didn't come to school until Wednesday. I barely saw her, since we had different schedules on Wednesday, but after the last period, I caught her at her locker.

"I can't talk right now." She jammed her last period books into the locker and pulled out her bookbag. "Kyle's picking me up. I'm supposed to be out front right at three o'clock."

I walked with her to the curb in front of the school. Kyle was already there. "Meet me in Mrs. A's garden," she whispered. "I'll come if I can."

I watched as Kyle leaned across the front seat and pushed the door open for Marleen. For a moment, he looked up at me, the only acknowledgement he seemed able to give me. I remembered how jealous I'd been of the way he'd looked at Tracy. I hated the way his eyes looked now, as if he'd never look at another girl that way again.

I went to Mrs. Whitford's garden and waited for Marleen. Brian cleared vines and weeds on the other side of the garden. I watched him for a while. He must have been digging in the dirt, too, because he left small black handprints on the clipper handles. When Marleen hadn't shown up after half an hour, I knew I had to go home. I left, going around the long way so I didn't pass the front of her house. I didn't want to know why she hadn't shown up, but when I got home, I found out anyway.

Mom stood on the front doorstep, and I noticed with surprise that David's car was in the drive. "Oh, thank God." Mom turned and yelled inside. "David, she's here!"

"What's the matter?" I had a hard time believing Mom would call David to come home just because I was half an hour late coming home from school.

David came around the corner. "Thank God." He hugged me, then pushed me back. "You had us worried, Charlie."

"Why?" My voice was muffled because Mom was hugging me now. I turned my head to catch a breath. "I'm only half an hour late."

"More like forty-five minutes," Mom sounded like she'd been crying. Her eyes were red.

"I was supposed to meet Marleen. I'm sorry I'm late." I noticed the glance they exchanged. "What happened?"

Another exchanged glance, then David stepped forward and put his arm around my shoulders. "They found Tracy, sweetheart." I felt his arm exert gentle pressure on my back. "Let's go inside and talk."

David didn't go back to work that afternoon. First they told me everything about Tracy. How two little four-year-old boys playing ball in the field behind Mr. Love's house had found her. Their moms were chatting in the kitchen when one of the boys overthrew the ball and the other went to chase it down. He saw something white in the tall grass and ran over to it, but instead of the ball, it was her elbow. Her red hair was tangled with the weeds, her face turned into the earth. David told me she was found naked, but somehow I couldn't imagine that. Everything else, but not that.

"How did she--" I couldn't finish the sentence.

David looked down at his hands. "She was murdered. Strangled." He hesitated, but I knew there was more. "And shot."

"Was she…" I took a deep breath. "Was she raped?"

David nodded. I saw his Adam's apple bob up and down as he swallowed. I knew that what had happened to Tracy had upset him deeply. "And that's why we have to talk to you."

David and Mom explained that we would have to have some new rules. Although they wouldn't sound fair at first, especially considering how much freedom I had always had, they were, in David and Mom's view, necessary. "You must come straight home from school," Mom said. "I want to know where you are at all times. If you want to go to a friend's house, I want you to tell me that morning so I know where you are. I want you to call me when you get there. And you must always be home before dark."

In light of what I'd just been told, this didn't sound so unreasonable. But the catch came next. Mom cleared her throat.

"And until further notice, I don't want you to go to Marleen's house after school."

"But Mom, you just said, if I called--"

"I know." Mom looked uncomfortable. "And Marleen is welcome here anytime. Anytime at all. I care about her, too. But I'm not sure her house is a, um, healthy environment for you right now."

"Healthy environment?" I fought between amazement and amusement. "What does that mean?"

"Just that until they catch whoever did this to Tracy, Marleen's family will be going through a lot." David's tone was gentle and measured, trying to soothe my ruffled feelings. "From all we understand, her brother is still a suspect, and though we love and care about Marleen, we don't know that much about the rest of her family."

"You mean they're not good enough for you." I glared at him, although I knew he was right. "You're such hypocrites. Marleen's family, especially Kyle, need people to believe in them right now. And Mom, you've known them for years. We need to be their friends right now. They need us to keep going, not act like anything is different."

Mom and David exchanged another glance. "We'll talk about it," Mom finally said with a sigh. "Maybe if you only went to Marleen's every now and then, and if you always let me know where you are…"

"It's not that we don't trust Marleen's family," David said. "It's just that with everything going on…and we want to be sure you are safe. That's our first priority."

"Right," I said. "And I will be. I've been friends with Marleen and her brothers for years. We can trust them."

"Of course you're right." Mom stroked my hair absently, and I wasn't even sure if she knew what she was saying.

## Chapter Ten

Marleen didn't talk about Tracy's murder over the next few weeks, but I knew life was rough for her family. The police called Kyle in for questioning twice before Christmas. Marleen's dad bought an answering machine for their telephone because reporters kept calling. Marleen told me to leave a message and if she was there listening, she'd pick up when I called. I felt weird calling and talking to a tape, but I did it.

Mom and David put up with my continued visits to Marleen's house, even though Marleen's family wasn't the same anymore. Kyle was home more often. In fact, he was home all the time except when he went to school or work, but he stayed in his room and seldom spoke to me or Marleen. Jeff actually seemed unchanged. Most of the time he stayed outside behind the metal building, smoking, unless he was tinkering on the Camaro.

Marleen's mom changed the most, though, and in the worst way. "She's not good with stress," Marleen said, but that seemed like an understatement to me. Mrs. Galloway seldom looked like she had makeup on, and sometimes she didn't look like she'd even combed her hair. She smelled a little funny, too. Marleen and I spent a lot of time in Mrs. Whitford's garden, and I stopped complaining about it since every time I saw Mrs. Galloway or Kyle, something in my chest hurt me. I wasn't anywhere near as frightened of creepy Brian as I was of the aura of despair in the Galloway house.

One day in December when it was too cold to stay outside, Marleen and I ventured into the house. Mrs. Galloway sat on the sofa, a glass with a little yellow liquid in it dangling from one hand, a lit cigarette in the other. I stopped in the doorway because I'd never seen Marleen's mother smoke or drink. I wasn't sure which way to look.

"Mom! I've got a friend over." Marleen flushed pink and gave me a miserable look.

"Forget it." Kyle spoke from the doorway to the kitchen. "She's too far gone. And I've gotta get to work. You two take over fire watch." He nodded at the lit cigarette.

When he left, I whispered to Marleen, "Is he still a suspect?"

Marleen just blinked at me, then stomped on the cigarette that had fallen on the beige carpet. "Let's go listen to some music."

In her bedroom, she put a cassette in her player and we lay on her bed for a while listening. "I miss Tracy." Her voice caught me off guard.

"What?" I knew what she had said, but I needed to buy myself some time. It was the first time Marleen had mentioned Tracy since her body had been found. "You miss her?"

"Yeah." Marleen exhaled heavily, as if she were relieved. "You know, when you and I weren't talking, Tracy was really nice to me. She even blew Kyle off once or twice to come up here with me and show me how to put on makeup or just to talk."

"She told me you missed me." I remembered that perfect fall day with the nip in the air and the wind rustling the dead leaves. "The last time I saw her, she told me. And she said I should call you."

"I'm glad she did." Marleen smiled at me, and in that instant we were uncomplicated best friends again. "Oh hey, that reminds me. What did you decide to do about your dad?"

For a second I thought she was talking about David. Then I remembered the slip of paper my mom had given me. The slip of paper with my father's address on it that I thought was so important just a few weeks ago. I hadn't touched it since the day Tracy disappeared.

"Nothing." I shrugged, looking up at the ceiling. "I mean, I haven't decided. In fact, I haven't even thought about it."

"Yeah," Marleen agreed. "Lots of other stuff going on, huh?"

We were silent for a while. Then Marleen said, "You know they wouldn't let Kyle go to the funeral?"

"Who?" I wasn't sure if she meant her parents or the police.

"Tracy's family." Her voice had a sharp edge. "They called and asked him to stay away. They said it was because of the reporters and stuff."

She fell silent again. I wondered if I should say something. Oh that's a shame? Would that be appropriate? When she spoke again, her tone was wistful. "He really wanted to go."

"Yeah. I guess he would."

Marleen sat up on the bed and looked at me earnestly. "I think it would have helped. I mean, he really misses her. And the police keep calling him a suspect. Dad says he shouldn't hire a lawyer, though. He says that would be just like admitting he's guilty."

"Really?"

"Yeah." She flopped back onto the bed, rolling over on her stomach and looking me straight in the eyes. "I think that's why Tracy's family didn't want him at the funeral, though. They think he's guilty."

"You don't though. Do you?" I asked, but Marleen didn't reply.

Marleen and her mom went to visit relatives in Chicago for Christmas. Two weeks off without my best friend left me without much to do for most of those unusually fine December days in the North Carolina mountains. Because I couldn't bear to be inside all the time, I started riding my bike a lot. I rode past Marleen's house as a matter of habit. Sometimes I'd see Kyle on his way out the door to work. I almost always saw Jeff near his tool shed. I never saw their dad anywhere around.

On the day after Christmas, I rode my bike past Marleen's house and paused outside Mrs. Whitford's garden. I stood on the silent street with my bike balanced between my legs and listened to the winter sounds I sometimes didn't even notice. Blue jays and crows calling to one another. The wind soughing softly in the top branches of the bare trees. A pinecone knocking against the needles of its tree as it fell from an upper branch. I didn't see Brian anywhere. In fact, both the Whitford and Galloway houses looked deserted. I was just about to continue on my way when another sound, a soft scuffing of leaves and pine needles, made me turn.

Jeff stood on the side of the road, a shovel in his hand. He nodded at me, then used the shovel to pick up something from the side of the road. Curious, I dismounted and pushed my bike over to see what it was.

The bloody mass on the shovel blade looked a little like spaghetti with gray fur mixed in. I could see the black beady eyes of the squirrel it had been, the mouth that was open in a grimace of pain. I made a face. "How did that happen?"

"Car." Jeff turned toward the house.

"What are you going to do with it?" I whispered, not sure if I wanted to know the answer.

He glanced over his shoulder. "Bury it."

My interest caught, I followed him. I'd never attended a funeral before, even one for a squirrel. "Can I come?"

Jeff shrugged. He led the way to the big oak tree in the corner of the Galloway yard. It bordered the Whitford property, and the soil surrounding its roots was rich and soft. I imagined those roots reaching down through the dirt for years and years, cutting it up and making it softer and softer.

A shallow pit gaped in the dark earth, and he dumped the squirrel into it. Then he reached with the shovel for the pile of dirt to cover the squirrel with. Horrified by the lack of ceremony, I held up a hand. "Wait."

Jeff looked on impatiently while I reached for a handful of dirt. A worm squirmed away from the light, burrowing deeper into the black soil. I had read in books that the sound of the first handful of dirt hitting the bottom of a grave is very final. I wanted to hear for myself.

With due solemnity, I held my hand over the grave and let the soil trickle out. It sounded like dirt hitting dirt. Maybe the sound wasn't very momentous because the squirrel and I hadn't known each other very well. Or maybe it was because there was no coffin, not even a shoebox, for the dirt to hit and create an echo. I thought of Tracy being buried in the cemetery. The thought made me feel a little foolish but I wasn't about to let on as I put the final touch to the little ceremony. "Rest in peace."

Jeff leaned on the shovel, looking at me with an expression between contempt and amusement. "You done?"

When I nodded, he finished shoveling the dirt over the grave and tamped it down. "My condolences," he said, but I noticed a twinkle in his eye as he shouldered the shovel and walked off to the metal building by the driveway.

On New Year's Eve, I rode to Marleen's house on my bike to see if I could find out when she'd be back. The sun shone in a clear, blue sky and the weatherman had said the high would be 65 degrees. I braked my bike in the drive when I saw Jeff basking on the hood of Kyle's Camaro. "Hey."

"Hey." Jeff didn't look around.

I leaned my bike against a tree and scuffed the toe of my sneaker into the gravel, exposing gray dirt beneath. "You heard from Marleen?"

"Mom called Dad last night. She said they'd be home day after tomorrow."

"Oh." I must've sounded sort of disappointed because Jeff looked at me then. I shrugged. "I was just sort of hoping she'd be home sooner. You know, so we could get together before school starts again."

"Right," Jeff turned back to his heavenly contemplations. Still lying on his back, he took a cigarette from his shirt pocket, a lighter from his jeans and lit the cigarette. He replaced the lighter and blew a smoke ring at the clouds. "You want to sit down?"

I hesitated. I could claim I had to get right back. But I didn't. Mom had loosened up a little over the holidays. She no longer seemed to think I was going to be carried off by a crazed serial killer. Plus, I'd made sure I followed the rules, letting her know where I was every moment. Over the past month, we'd grown used to what had happened to Tracy. It no longer shocked us the way it had at first, and that was both sad and a relief.

If Marleen had been around, I never would have considered Jeff's invitation. In fact, I never would have even spoken to Jeff. But Marleen was gone, and I was lonely. And the warm hood of the Camaro looked inviting. Before I quite knew what I was doing, Jeff had scooted over and I had slid up onto the Camaro next to him. I hesitated about lying down, though.

"Won't we get in trouble?"

He exhaled and glanced at me. "No. I change the oil. The car is part mine, and Kyle knows it. I just don't have my license yet."

Jeff's reply shocked me a little. That was the most he'd spoken in my presence, ever, at least within my memory. It also put Kyle's bossiness in a different light. "Cool." I lay back next to him.

The metal of the hood warmed our backs through our sweaters. Jimmy Buffett played on the car stereo, singing of beaches where there was no winter. With my eyes closed, I could almost imagine I was there. And when I opened my eyes, Jeff was there, spitting smoke rings at the sky. I could feel his shoulder against mine. He smelled a little like motor oil, and a lot like cigarette smoke. I thought it was a very surreal way to spend the last day of the year.

Feeling awkward, I decided to start a conversation. "How's Kyle?"

Jeff exhaled, blowing a column of smoke up at the sky. "Figures," he muttered. Then he said, as if he were reciting lines for a school play, "Kyle is as well as can be expected for an innocent young man whose future is being ruined by false accusations. Why, he can't even leave town!"

He sounded so much like his mother did when she was sober that I couldn't help laughing. Kyle's mom's tirades had become well known on the streets of our town. At the grocery store, the dry cleaners, or just walking out to the mailbox, if she encountered someone foolish enough to ask about her family, she had the audience she required. Jeff smiled at my reaction. For a moment, he looked like he thought he was pretty hot stuff. I grinned. "It's been pretty tough, huh?"

"Sorta." He sobered again and looked back at the sky. "It's worse for the rest of them, really. Mom's taken it hard. Kyle's her golden boy, the one who's going to be somebody. He's supposed to get a scholarship for college, but if he's arrested…" His voice trailed off.

"Marleen told me," I said. "He won't be arrested, though."

"How come?" Jeff's mouth became a twisted little smile that made me feel naïve.

"'Cause he didn't do it. How can they arrest him?"

"Oh, they could arrest him," Jeff said, and though it occurred to me that he hadn't specified whether Kyle could be arrested because he did it or for some other reason, I chose not to ask any more.

The next day I returned to Marleen's house. The Camaro wasn't in the drive this time, but I parked my bike next to the metal shed and walked around behind it. Jeff sat on the concrete block wall, his feet dangling in the dead weeds, a cigarette in his mouth. It wasn't quite as warm as the day before had been.

"Happy New Year," I said.

"Yeah, you too." He didn't look at me. He seemed to be studying the metal wall in front of him.

I sat and looked at the rusted surface of the metal building. I couldn't think of anything to say, and I wondered why. We'd talked easily enough yesterday, lying on the hood of the Camaro looking at the sky. I'd felt sort of free yesterday, but today that feeling was gone. I felt stiff and wooden and stupid. Why had I come? Jeff didn't want me there. And I didn't care. I didn't even like him.

"Want one?" Jeff offered his cigarette.

"No," I said, too fast so I added, "thanks."

He shrugged. “Marleen’ll be back tomorrow.”

“Yeah.”

“Guess you guys’ll be over in Mrs. A’s garden drooling over Brian boy, then?”

“Gross.” I made a face.

He smiled. “Yeah.”

Feeling I was on a roll, I added, “He’s creepy.”

“Marleen likes him.”

“Well, I don’t.” I shivered a little as a breeze stirred the dead, dry grass at my feet. “I don’t know what she sees in him.”

“He makes her feel important. Or she thinks he does, anyway.”

“She says he’s an artist.” I paused, wondering for the first time about this statement. “How would she know?”

“You kidding me?” He snorted. “She’s over there every afternoon, talking to him. You would think he was a high school kid instead of a middle aged man.”

“Yeah, but he wants to talk to her, too, right? Why’s he so interested in her?”

Jeff shrugged. “She needs to be careful.” He crushed out his cigarette butt, his eyes wandering over to Mrs. Whitford’s garden. From where we sat, we could only see a few shrubs and the tops of the trees. “If he gets her back in that house without anyone around…”

“Or even just back in the garden. I tried to warn her. But you don’t think he’d do anything, really, do you?” I shivered again. I'd heard stories of girls being taken advantage of by older men before. And Tracy. Tracy was always there to remind me of the darker part of society, the part nobody talked about.

Jeff shrugged. "I'll talk to her."

"It won't do any good." I had started to feel panicky. "She won't listen. Maybe you should tell your mom--" I remembered the shape his mother had been in the last time I saw her "--or your dad."

"You know that's not a good idea. At least you know it won't do any good to tell my mom. And you don't know my dad." He paused and frowned. "And you should be glad you don't."

I felt another chill. "It's cold today." I pulled my sweater closer to my neck.

"No colder than any other day," Jeff said, lighting another cigarette.

## Chapter Eleven

Marleen didn't call me when she got home the next day. Jeff had told me she'd be home in the morning. I waited until mid afternoon, then I called her. "Hey, what's up?" I tried not to sound hurt that she hadn't called me right away.

"Oh, hello, Charlie." Marleen yawned. "I was just unwinding. It was such a long flight from Chicago."

"Yeah, I guess so. About two hours, wasn't it?"

"At least three." Marleen sounded put out that she had to qualify that for me. "Maybe three and a half. And add to that the time we spent in the airport. Why, I've been up since six o'clock this morning."

"Oh," I said.

"Yes," Marleen said. "I think I'm going to take a nap now, Charlie. I've just finished unpacking, and I want to be fresh for school tomorrow."

"Sure. I mean, I guess…" Fresh for school? What did that mean?

"So, hopefully we'll run into each other in the hall, then. Or perhaps I'll see you for lunch." Marleen hung up, leaving me wondering what had happened to my best friend.

I rode my bike over to Marleen's, anyway. Jeff was playing stickball with a couple of black kids from the neighborhood. I sat on the hood of the Camaro and watched.

“What are you doing here?” Marleen’s voice made me jump.

“Oh, hey.” I shrugged. “I thought you were taking a nap.”

“I looked out my window to tell my idiot brother to be quiet and saw you.” Marleen looked suspicious. “So what’s up?”

I hesitated. I had several options. I could tell the truth, that I came to see Jeff. I could lie and say I was hoping she’d come out. Or I could opt for the ridiculous and say I was a fan of stickball. I didn’t see myself winning, no matter what. At that moment, the ball landed at my feet and I looked at it dumbly.

Jeff jogged over to retrieve the ball, frowning. “Maybe she didn’t come to see you, butthead. I doubt she wants to have to listen to your tales of life in the big city.” He looked at me. “She’s been telling us about living in the fast lane ever since she got home this morning.”

“Well, who else is she going to come see? You?” Marleen sneered. “Don’t flatter yourself.” She glanced at me, expecting me to share the laughter, but when I glanced away, she must have realized what was up. She rolled her eyes. “Oh geez, if you can’t have one brother, the other will do, huh? I’m starting to think you never really wanted to be my friend.”

“Marleen,” I grabbed her arm, but she pulled away.

“I’m going back to bed.” She turned back toward her house, shaking her head and waving a hand at me. “Have a ball.”

Jeff shot her a bird, then turned to me. “You want to play?” I hesitated only a moment before joining the game.

As I rode my bike home after the stickball game, I realized it had been a long time since I'd had that much fun. Marleen seldom wanted to play ball or ride bikes anymore. She talked a lot about art and her newfound love of nature. I thought of her running from Mrs. Whitford's garden swatting at a bee and laughed, almost running off the road. Then I sighed. Marleen and I had been friends for a long time. I didn't like the thought that we had different interests now. Especially if one of Marleen's interests was Brian Whitford.

The media had lost interest in Tracy's death. The headlines were about taxes and gas prices and the mayor. "The trail's getting cold," David said. "They figure there won't be an arrest anytime real soon."

Maybe that was it, or maybe the loss of newspaper headlines had to do with the fact that our tiny town had a newspaper with five reporters, total. That number included Sam Prescott who covered the high school sports teams and Lulu Grover who visited the local restaurants as the "Mystery Diner". There was no hard-boiled crime reporter to take a real interest in the case, and the remaining three reporters had no experience covering murder stories. Probably, I thought, they figured if the police chief didn't call them, there was no story to report.

So I was totally unprepared to see David open the paper on a Saturday late in January to a banner headline that read

"Local Girl's Death Unsolved, Boyfriend Still a Suspect". The article, which David read aloud to Mom and me, rehashed Tracy's death, the days after her disappearance and the police investigation. Listening to the story was almost worse than reliving the actual event. All I could think about was how Kyle and his family would feel reading this.

"Why would they do this?" I asked. "Why would they bring it all back again when there's nothing new to report?"

David shook his head and Mom took a sip of her coffee. She patted my hand absently, but the gesture didn't make me feel any better.

Over the next few weeks, Marleen mixed Chicago and Brian Whitford liberally in her conversation, but would talk of little else. She never wanted to come home with me, although she invited me over as often as usual. "Brian's an artist," she told me. "He wants to paint me. He says the way my hair traps the light is exquisite. He studies beauty, you know, that's why he works in his father's garden so much."

"Really?" I knew from experience that saying "gross", which was what I felt, would only get me ignored. I didn't want to be ignored. I wanted to get through to Marleen that what she was doing was stupid.

Marleen studied her fingernails. "I know you think Brian's too old for me."

"What?" I sat up.

"Love knows no age," Marleen said. "And besides, our souls are the same age."

Oh crap. "What?"

"That's what Brian says. He believes in reincarnation. He says everyone's soul is the same age. We were all created at the same time, it's just we get placed on the earth at different times."

Sounded like a bunch of bull to me. But my fear for my friend got the better of me. "Marleen, he's not trying to get you to do … anything, is he?"

Marleen smirked. "Like what?" When I hesitated, she laughed again. "You don't even know, do you? What men and women do when they're in love?"

"Of course, I do." I felt confident here. My mom had told me the process the year before, when she was pregnant. We'd both been uncomfortable and a lot of the stuff she'd told me, I'd already known, but we went through the motions, anyway.

"Right," Marleen said. "In theory, maybe. I guess your mom explained it to you."

"How much more do you know, then?" I demanded.

"Plenty." She put her hands over her head and stretched. I noticed her breasts, which had been mere nubs before she left for Chicago, had grown respectably. I looked away.

"If what you know you learned from Brian, you can keep it." I spoke as decisively as I could. I heard a door slam and knew Brian was on his way out to do his afternoon gardening. I peered above the bushes. Brian had evidently decided to take a smoking break before starting his afternoon chores. I watched as he put the cigarette to his lips. His small hand looked more natural on the small white cylinder than it did on the more substantial handle of a shovel or clippers. He drew a deep breath off the cigarette and I watched as his whole body relaxed, as if he enjoyed the nicotine with his whole body, not just his mouth and lungs. I heard Marleen give a little longing sigh beside me. "I'm leaving now." I didn't bother disguising my disgust.

"See you," Marleen said, already heading for the fence near the storage shed. I watched as she approached Brian. He was tying a pair of dirty boots, propping his foot on the old stone steps from the house. She must have spoken because he turned and smiled. Then he straightened and came over to the fence. His pale fingers closed on one of the posts like a spider with too-short legs. To my horror, he looked over her shoulder and saw me, raising his hand in a half-wave, half-beckon. I waved quickly as I turned and practically ran away.

Coming out of the garden, I nearly ran into Kyle and stumbled backward quickly. "Oh, sorry." I stopped to catch my breath.

"Yeah," he said, looking not at me, but into the distance beyond the garden. "Watch out back here, Charlie."

He wandered away, his hands in his pockets. I stared after him, wondering what he was warning me to watch out for. Him? The snakes and bugs hadn't woken from their winter's rest yet, though we'd had a few warmer days. February was unpredictable. One day might be sunny and warm, the next cold and gray. On the warm days, the sun reached down into the soil and drew out tiny buds and triangles of green that would become daffodils and crocuses in a few weeks. But on the bitter cold days that still outnumbered the sunny warm ones, the wind and sometimes freezing rain battered the little fronds back down.

"He lost his job." I turned to see Jeff perched on the old swing set. "Kyle did. I guess you're wondering why he's wandering around talking to himself."

"Yeah." I sat next to him. "What's up? What're you doing back here?"

"Watching there." Jeff gestured with his cigarette at the garden.

I nodded. I knew what he meant. I wanted to see Marleen come out of the garden, too. "She's talking to him now."

Jeff smoked his cigarette in silence. We swung in minuscule arcs, suspended in air by the rusty old chains that squeaked and squawked above us. A hawk circled above the garden, looking for food in the undergrowth below. I imagined a tiny mouse venturing from his burrow, hoping for a little early food, seeds and the like. From beneath the overhanging leaves, weeds and bushes, he'd have no clue what danger awaited above.

"Why did Kyle lose his job?" I finally asked.

"His boss figures having Kyle working there is making business fall off. Like we have any other record store in town to go to." Jeff looked disgusted.

"I guess he's had a lot to worry about," I said. "Kyle, I mean."

"Dad hired a lawyer. Yesterday. Word is, the police department wants to make an arrest soon." Jeff clenched his teeth tightly over the cigarette. I wondered if he realized how much he was smoking.

I remembered the headlines in the papers a few weeks before. "They're worried about what the newspaper will say, aren't they?"

"Mom says they should be looking for a black man." He said it matter-of-factly, but I noticed a strain in his voice. I glanced at him. He dropped his cigarette in the dirt and leaned over on the swing, still swaying back and forth, but also grinding the cigarette butt into the dirt with the toe of his boot.

I looked away, at Mrs. Whitford's garden, and something reminded me of the day Tracy's body was found. I remembered watching Brian working in the garden. Weeding, cutting, pruning, digging. He'd left his tools lined up outside the shed, and they cast black shadows on the white wall behind them. I remembered the black dirt on them in the shape of tiny black handprints.

## Chapter Twelve

I dreamt about Brian. I was in the garden looking for my watch. For some reason I was sure Brian had buried it in the garden. If I could only find the right place to dig. I burrowed under the rose bushes, in the flower beds, under the magnolia tree. Each time, I only got a few inches down before I realized how many more places I had to search and, feeling frantic, I leapt on to the next place. My shirt hung dirty and stained on my shoulders. I knew I would never be clean again. “Are you looking for this?” Brian asked. I turned to find him holding my watch in his small, dirt-stained hands.

I woke screaming. Mom came running. David hurried to calm the baby who’d woken to my cry. Mom held me. David stood in the doorway as I sobbed. It was the fifth night in a row that the dream had disturbed us all.

The next morning, Saturday, I came down late to find Mom and David still sitting at the breakfast table. The baby played in the living room, rolling over on his back to touch each toe, then getting up on all fours to crawl around in circles. Mom had put the gates up, so he couldn’t get out of the living room, which was completely baby-proofed. No escape, baby. I yawned.

“Sit down, Charlie.” Mom sounded more tired than I felt. “I’ll get your cereal for you.”

I sat, but I knew something was up. "I'm sorry I woke you guys again last night."

David reached across the table and covered my hand with his. "We want to talk to you about that, sweetie."

Mom set my cereal down in front of me, then sat across from me next to David, who looked at me with sympathy. "It's not your fault, Charlie. We think you have some unresolved feelings about Tracy."

Mom watched me eat my cereal in silence for several minutes. When I set aside my spoon and reached for my juice, she glanced at David and then faced me. "Can you tell us a little more about your dream? It doesn't sound terrifying, but it obviously means something pretty horrific to you.""

I'd been very nonspecific, only telling her that in my dream someone was hiding something from me and I was trying to find it. Although I had a pretty good idea about the meaning of my dream, I didn't want to talk about it. Just the thought made me sick to my stomach. Besides, could I tell my parents I thought Brian had been the one who murdered Tracy? Wasn't that false accusation or something? What if they called the police and the police wanted to know why I suspected Brian? If I told them about Marleen, I'd be betraying her, and I didn't want to do that. Plus, it didn't prove anything. Even if Brian was a pervert, it didn't mean he was a murderer, did it?

I bit my lip and looked at the newspaper lying on the table. “I think David’s right. I’m pretty sure it has to do with Tracy.”

David nodded. “That’s why we want you to talk to someone, Charlie. Someone who can help you sort things out, decide what to do with all your feelings.”

I frowned at him. “I’m not dumb. You mean a shrink.”

“A therapist,” Mom said. “Not a psychiatrist. You’re not sick, Charlie. Nothing’s wrong with you. But you might still have a lot of fear and anger about Tracy’s death that you don’t even know about.”

Oh, I knew about it, all right. I could see no good way to get out of this one, so I shrugged. “Okay. I doubt it’ll do much good, but if you want to pay somebody to talk to me, that’s fine.”

“Sometimes it helps to talk, Charlie,” David said. “And maybe it’ll be easier to talk to a therapist than to us.”

Mom shivered, wrapping her robe tighter around herself. “I wish they’d just catch whoever did it. We’d all sleep better then.”

But I wondered if we would. Now that such an ugly thing had happened in our quiet little town, the damage was done. Unlike a fire or hurricane or tornado, the damage wasn’t physical and couldn’t be seen, but I felt sure that everyone who lived there was a little less trusting, more likely to lock their doors at night, more suspicious of strangers. And once that trust was lost and the door locking began, there was no going back. Though catching the murderer might make us feel better temporarily, we'd never be the same town again.

"Ahhh!" the baby shrieked, standing at the gate. I looked up and he grinned, his four tiny teeth shiny white in his mouth. I grinned back and he held a block between the bars of the gate. David and Mom laughed, and I took the block and patted the baby on his head as I went over to put my cereal bowl in the sink.

Mom took me to my first therapy appointment on the following Wednesday. I was still having the dreams, though I was no longer waking everyone with my screams. Still, I think Mom knew. I left Mom in the waiting room staring at a bowl of fake violets swimming through a sea of magazines on the coffee table.

The therapist, Mrs. Godfrey, wanted me to tell her about my dream, but she didn't want to have to ask me straight out. She sat at her desk and tapped a pencil eraser on a yellow legal pad. "So, your mother tells me you've been having nightmares."

" A nightmare." I focused on the black and white clock on the wall behind her. It had a red second hand that swept smoothly around the circumference of the clock's perfect circle every minute.

Mrs. Godfrey made a note. The red second hand began another sweep without ever pausing after the first one. I wondered how many minutes long a session was. "Would you like to talk about the dream, dear?" Mrs. Godfrey didn't look like the type who should be calling a teenage girl "dear". Her hair was smooth and yellow, but there was something hard about her face, as though there were too many angles.

"Not really." I tried to figure out how many triangles I could make out of her face.

"That's fine. You don't have to talk about anything you don't want to." She pretended to be consulting her notes. "Why don't you start, then?"

"What?" I couldn't figure what she wanted from me.

Mrs. Godfrey gave me a sharp look over the top of her notebook. "Why don't you ask me a question? Perhaps something about the therapy?"

I couldn't think of anything to ask. Mrs. Godfrey's suggestion made me pause for thought as the second hand made another circular sweep. Finally, I asked, "What good is this going to do?"

"Good?" Mrs. Godfrey raised her eyebrows.

"Yeah," I said. "I mean, will it make the nightmare stop? If I tell you about it?"

Mrs. Godfrey pursed her lips, causing valleys and hills in her lipstick. I noticed her lipstick was the same color as the red second hand on the clock. "Well, I hope that eventually we will be able to make some sense out of your dream together. I hope I will be able to help you do that. It may be something that is worrying you, something that has been worrying you for some time. Maybe it's something you feel you need to take care of or something you're afraid of."

"How could something I'm worrying about affect my dreams?"

Mrs. Godfrey smiled. Maybe she smiled because she thought my question was innocent. Maybe she was just trying to reassure me. Either way, it irritated me. "Our dreams are our thoughts and feelings trying to speak to us. It's a way our mind tries to stay healthy. If we bury a worry or a fear because we don't want to think about it, or if we just ignore something because we don't want to deal with it, our mind can use our dreams to remind us that this isn't healthy."

Her words made me stop to think before I asked my next question. "Why isn't it healthy? Could I get sick?"

"That's why your nightmare is so bad," Mrs. Godfrey said. "Your brain is reminding you that you have something important you need to work out. You need to pay attention to it."

"After that, she gave me a dream journal and told me to write down my dreams before the next session," I told Jeff later that day. We sat on the concrete block wall beside his driveway. All along the wall, a line of daffodils nodded their sunny heads. I loved daffodils. They looked like they thought of themselves as royalty, but they bloomed in the most common of places. Like Jeff's wall, which was the same color as the sky. Dirty slate gray mud puddles in the middle of the gravel drive reflected the sky back at itself. It seemed the daffodils were the only bright things in the universe.

Jeff looked dubious. "What good will that do?"

I grinned. "I asked the same thing. She says the more detail I can remember about my dreams, the better chance I'll have of figuring out what my mind is trying to tell me."

Jeff shook his head. He absently nudged the head of a top-heavy daffodil with one toe of his sneaker. "Is this just for the nightmare or all your dreams?"

For some reason, his question made me blush. Over the past several weeks, Jeff and I had become good friends again due to Marleen's absence and preoccupation with Brian. Still, it felt odd to talk about my dreams with him, sort of too intimate for friends to share. "All of them." I lowered my eyes and watched him play with the daffodil. I found another one with my toe and pushed it gently, watching it spring back up again.

"Did she know what the nightmare meant?"

I shrugged. "I didn't tell her about it."

"Why not?"

"I dunno." I felt uncomfortable. "I haven't told anyone all about it."

"Tell me." Jeff took out a cigarette and lit it. He inhaled deeply, then pushed the smoke back out of his lungs. "Hurry up, I gotta go clean out the gutters."

"Let me try it." I pointed at the cigarette.

"Why?"

"I just want to try it." I didn't add that I didn't want to tell him about my nightmare. I didn't want to tell anybody. I wanted the nightmares to stop, and I wanted to be wrong. I didn't want Marleen to be in danger. But I did want to feel that sensation of relaxation that Jeff--and even Brian--seemed to get whenever he drew the smoke deep into his lungs.

"You've never wanted to try it before." Jeff looked suspicious.

"There's a first time for everything." I beckoned. "C'mon, let me try."

"You sure you want to try?" Jeff held the slim white cylinder between his thumb and forefinger. It was obvious he'd been doing this a while, and again I wondered if he realized how much he'd been smoking.

"Yeah, gimme it."

He took another long draw on the cigarette, his eyes sparkling wickedly at me. Then he leaned forward and kissed me. His lips tasted like nicotine and bubble gum. I wondered when he chewed bubble gum. I smelled the metallic scent of motor oil again. As our lips touched and lingered and he lightly caressed the side of my face, I sucked in a deep breath of him and held it in my lungs as he pulled away.

Jeff took another drag on the cigarette before crushing it and tossing it into a can full of butts. "You don't need this." He jumped off the wall and headed up the sidewalk to his house.

I wasn't sure what to think. Jeff had caught me off guard with his kiss, and though it hadn't been unpleasant, it was not exactly what I'd imagined my first kiss would be. My confused feelings reminded me of something else as I pedaled for home. Something I'd nearly forgotten about. I parked my bike in the garage so David wouldn't have a hard time getting his car in, went inside and up to my room. I took my little music box off my dresser and sat down on the bed.

Inside was the envelope. Inside the envelope was the slip of paper with my father's name and address on it. A layer of jewelry box and a layer of paper was all that separated me from the knowledge I'd thought I needed. But since my mother had given it to me, I hadn't opened the envelope to look at the name. Although I had it within my grasp, I hadn't looked close enough to know what my own father's name was. I hadn't even taken it out of the jewelry box.

I imagined myself taking the slip of paper out, reading the name and address, sitting down and writing a letter to the man I'd never known. Then I imagined myself taking the paper out and crumpling it up unread, or, more imaginatively, making a boat out of newspaper and placing the folded slip of paper on it like a sailor. Then I'd take it down to the pond and set it afloat. None of it seemed right, so I left the paper in my music box and went down to the pond.

Mom sat on the bench beside the pond. I sat beside her. "Where's the baby?"

"He has a name." Her voice sounded a little sharper than usual.

"Where's Dougie?" Douglas seemed like too adult of a name for such a little guy. I always called him Dougie, and so did David.

"Asleep." She tossed a rock into the pond. We watched the uneventful ripples. No turtles raised their heads from the depths like sea monsters to disrupt the smooth water.

I summoned my courage. "What's up?"

"Oh nothing." Mom sighed and wiped her palms on her legs. "You know Thursday is David's and my anniversary." I had forgotten, but I nodded like I remembered. "I'd just hoped we could go out for a nice dinner, but I can't find a sitter."

"I'll watch Dougie." I felt older and much more mature than I had that morning.

Mom shook her head. "The sitter's partly for you."

"I don't need a babysitter. I'll watch Dougie; we'll be fine." Confused by my mother's attitude and emboldened by Jeff's kiss, I felt sure I was right.

"Charlie, don't give me a hard time about this. We'll just go out some other time." She got up and went into the house.

I shrugged and turned back to the pond. I could see our house reflected upside down in the pond, complete with shrubs and trees and nodding daffodils. I wondered what life was like in the upside down house. If I brought my father's name out here and set it afloat in its newspaper boat, would it reach an upside down me? And would the upside down me know what to do with it?

That night I dreamt I was sitting in Mrs. Whitford's garden. Unlike other dreams of the garden, I was at peace. I wasn't looking for anything because there was nothing to search for. The roses bloomed in red and white and yellow. Someone walked toward me. It wasn't Brian, though. It was Jeff and I noticed again the green tints in his blue eyes. I smiled at him and he held out a rose to me.

I woke with a start and glanced at the dream journal. Then I rolled over and sought the dream again. I had a feeling I didn't have to worry about Brian stealing anything from me again.

## Chapter Thirteen

"What's the saddest thing that's ever happened to you?" Jeff asked me the next day as we sat on the wall.

Had anything sad ever really happened to me? I never knew my grandparents. I'd never had any pets because Mom was allergic, so I'd never dealt with death at all. If he meant sad by omission, those would count. So would my dad being gone. But Jeff meant something more dramatic. The only thing I could think of was Sherry.

In first grade, my best friend Sherry found out her mother was dying. For some reason, Sherry's mom wanted to sail around the world, so Sherry left school and went to sail around the world with her mother and stepfather. We wrote letters to each other for a little while. Sherry drew me pictures of some of the things she saw on the trip (mostly seagulls and sailboats, but once she sent me a picture of a white sandy beach with a little straw hut). Then Sherry's mom died and Sherry came home to live with her real father. I was thrilled at first to have my friend back. But Sherry was different from how she was before the trip. She got in big fights with her dad all the time and she ran away once. Then Sherry's stepfather came and took her away and Sherry never wrote to me again.

When I told Jeff about Sherry, he said, "Where was the beach with the straw hut?"

"I don't know." Until he mentioned it, I hadn't felt the loss of that knowledge.

"You should see if you could find it. Someday. Anyway, that wasn't really that sad, at least the part that happened to you." He picked up a stick and began stripping the bark away, exposing the white skin beneath. "Pretty sad for Sherry, but not for you."

"How do you mean?" I tried not to feel a little jealous that he felt sympathetic for a girl he'd never met and who I hadn't seen in years,

He shrugged. "Well, put yourself in her shoes. She loses her mom, the guy she thinks of as her dad has to give her up and she doesn't like her real dad. Actually, it's pretty sad for her real dad, too, if you think about it. I guess you've led a more sheltered life than I thought if that's the saddest thing that's ever happened to you."

"Fine." I knew I sounded defensive. "What's the saddest thing that ever happened to you?"

"When I was five, I found my grandfather dead in his house."

"Really?" I immediately regretted challenging him. "That's awful."

"He'd been dead for a while. Mom sent me over to check on him when he didn't answer his phone. He just lived down the road." He took out a pocketknife and began to whittle the stick. "It was summer. I remember hearing the bullfrogs in the pond behind his house. And there were crickets everywhere. But although I remember all of that, and I even remember that the screen door squeaked when I went inside, I can't remember finding him."

"I guess you don't really want to remember that." I thought of my last therapy session. "Mrs. Godfrey says our brains protect us from bad memories."

"Probably." He looked thoughtful. "How's that going, anyway? The therapy."

I sighed. "I dunno. She keeps wanting me to talk about the nightmare. But I don't even have it anymore."

"What was it, anyway?"

I thought about it, then decided it was okay to tell Jeff about the nightmare. I certainly wouldn't tell him about my other dreams, though--the ones he was in. And so I told him about losing my watch in Mrs. Whitford's garden. And about digging for it, black earth all around me. Then seeing Brian, covered in filth, holding the watch up and asking me if I was looking for it.

"I have no idea what it means," I said.

Jeff was silent. He held the pocketknife in one hand and the whittled stick in the other. When he looked at me, I felt like his eyes, which were as blue as they'd been in my dream, could look right through me. "Do you think Brian Whitford killed Tracy?"

I didn't know how to answer. I wasn't sure what the truth was myself. I only knew for sure that Brian Whitford scared me. "I--he scares me," I admitted. "But I don't have any proof he ever did anything wrong. But that's why I didn't want Marleen to hang out with him."

Jeff folded the pocketknife and put it and the stick in his pocket. Then he put his arm around me. I was surprised to realize I was trembling. "You may know more than you think," he said. "Your dream may really mean something. Maybe you're trying to remember something you've blocked, like me with my grandpa's death."

I leaned against him, glad for his arm around me even while part of me hoped Marleen wasn't watching from her bedroom window. "But what? There's nothing to remember. The only time I saw him after Tracy disappeared was one afternoon when Marleen asked me to meet her in the garden." I stopped and drew in a startled breath. In my mind I saw Brian's small hands on the clipper handles, leaving black handprints. My mind's eye saw them clearer than my real eyes had. Caked under the nails was something red, like blood, even.

"Blood?" Jeff sat up straighter, his arm falling from my shoulders. "Are you sure?"

"Yes! And oh, Jeff, it was the day they found Tracy! Maybe he dumped the body that day. Maybe he forgot to wash his hands." I was excited. I jumped up. "We have to call the police."

Jeff shook his head. "We can't call the police."

"Why not?" I glared at him. "Think of Kyle! The police need to catch the real killer, but they're likely to arrest Kyle any day. And Marleen! She could be in a lot of danger!"

Jeff shook his head again, spreading his hands in a helpless gesture. "I know, but what are we going to tell them? That you just remembered that on a day like almost four months ago you saw Brian Whitford with blood under his fingernails? It's pretty farfetched, and I'm even suspicious of the guy." He hesitated. "Maybe we could make an anonymous telephone call, though. Just say that he did it and suggest they check him out."

"Great! Let's do it!" I started up the walk, but Jeff caught my arm.

"I'll do it. Mom's … asleep. Wait here." He sprinted up the walk.

I did, pacing back and forth. As I waited, Marleen emerged from Mrs. Whitford's garden. I hadn't even realized she was there.

She paused and smirked at me. "Oh, I see you're here. Waiting for my brother? Have you decided which one you like best yet?"

"Marleen! You'll never guess what Jeff and I just figured out. We know who killed Tracy."

"Really? I thought everybody knew that by now. It was my brother." She turned and swept up the steps while I gaped at her.

A moment later, when Jeff came down the steps, I was still standing there with my mouth open. "I did it," he said, and I snapped my mouth closed.

"What did they say?" I spoke in a whisper without even intending to.

"They asked who I was and I hung up."

"How will we know if they take the call seriously?" I looked over my shoulder at the Whitford house. "Are you sure they understood you?"

Jeff frowned at me. "Of course they understood me. I told them if they wanted to catch Tracy Collins's killer, they should check out Brian Whitford. Pretty clear, I think." He looked up at the Whitford house. "Let's go watch."

I hesitated. "I'm not sure. I should go. Mom and David have their anniversary tonight and I was going to help Mom with dinner."

"C'mon." Jeff seized my hand. "Just for a few minutes. I bet they'll send somebody out right away."

I gave in. We snuck through the garden to a corner behind some bushes. We crouched behind the bushes and watched. After a while, I shifted my weight and sat in some pine needles. "I don't think they're coming."

Jeff sat next to me. "Give them time. They probably don't have anybody out here, you know."

At that moment a patrol car pulled up to the curb in front of the Whitford house. I squealed and Jeff grabbed me, putting his hand over my mouth and pulling me back into the bushes. He smiled at my outraged expression, took his hand away and replaced it with his mouth. The kiss lasted longer and Jeff tasted different. More bubblegum. Minty. When he drew away from my second kiss ever, I whispered, “You’re not smoking anymore.”

Jeff smiled again, still holding me against him, and looked back at the Whitford house as Brian opened the door and the police officer spoke quietly to him. We listened to the low murmur of voices, then the officer went inside.

“This could take a while.” Jeff released me and pulled out his pocketknife, starting to whittle again. “You could go home and I’ll call you later.”

“Okay.” Much as I wanted to stay, I knew I didn’t dare. “Jeff.” He looked up. I hesitated, not sure what I wanted to say. “I, um, be careful?”

He nodded. “I’ll call you.”

We ate in the dining room. Dinner had never lasted so long. I kept glancing at the telephone. Not only did I want to know what had happened, but Jeff’s phone call would mark the first time a boy had every willingly dialed my number. I hoped he remembered it so he wouldn’t have to ask Marleen.

“Don’t you agree, Charlie?” Mom’s voice startled me out of my reverie.

"What?" I snapped back to the table. Mom had made a roast, boiled white potatoes and carrots, green beans, Parker House rolls and a pecan pie for dessert. I hadn't been able to swallow a bite.

Mom frowned at me. "I said this has been one of the best years of our lives, don't you agree?"

"Oh, sure," I nodded. "We love you, David." I must have sounded a little less than enthusiastic because David laughed out loud and Mom groaned.

"What's wrong with you, anyway? You've been looking at that telephone every other second. Are you expecting a call?"

"Mom, really." I rolled my eyes. I wouldn't have admitted to them for anything that I was expecting a phone call from a boy, even though I knew it was hardly one of the seven deadly sins.

The phone rang.

"I'll get it." I jumped up, but David was closer and grabbed it with a sort of a wicked grin, holding me off with one hand.

"Hello … Sure, I'll get her…May I ask who's calling, please?" And then, although I was standing two feet away with my hand out, he held the receiver a foot above his head and bellowed, "Charlie! There's a boy on the phone for you! It's Jeff!"

I jumped and snatched the phone from his hand while he and Mom collapsed into their dinner plates, giggling. "Thanks a lot, guys." I stretched the phone cord as far as it would go so I could get into the kitchen and close the door. I leaned against the door and breathed deeply before I spoke. "Sorry, my dad thinks he's being funny."

"No problem." Jeff sounded amused.

I yanked the cord a little further away from the dining room door and sat with my back against the wall under the kitchen calendar. Mom and David would linger over dinner for another half hour, I knew. Then they'd probably have a glass of wine in front of the fire. "Okay, what happened?"

"They arrested him." Jeff's next sentence stopped me as I jumped up to celebrate. "But not for Tracy's murder. For corrupting a minor."

"What?" I felt like a balloon with a hole in it, slowly giving up air. I collapsed back to the floor.

"They found paintings of Marleen in his house." Jeff sighed. I pictured him rubbing the back of his head in frustration. I wished I was there to smooth his hair back down. "She's been posing nude for him."

"Oh God." For a minute I could think of nothing else to say. I looked at the reflection of the room in the dark window. I listened to Jeff's breathing and smelled the pot roast wafting in from the dining room. I hadn't finished my dinner, but I didn't think I'd ever be hungry again.

"Mom and Dad have taken Marleen to the station to make a statement. I won't know anything more until they get back."

"Was she okay?" Despite my friend's recent lack of interest in my life, I was still concerned about her.

"She was crying and screaming at them. She thinks she's in love with him." He fell silent. "Dad slapped her. He called her a whore and a whole lot of other stuff." Again, the stark tone of his voice shocked me. I found myself wishing we hadn't found out about Marleen and Brian. I didn't want to know. I didn't want to hear that pain in Jeff's voice.

"Oh Jesus, I'm so sorry," I whispered. "I had no idea…"

"It's okay, Charlie." Jeff paused again. "It was hard to watch, but you may have saved my sister from a lot."

"Do you think they'll be able to arrest him for killing Tracy?"

"I dunno." Jeff sounded doubtful. "I mean, we don't know he did it, do we? Maybe you were scared of Brian for a different reason. This reason. It's possible he had nothing to do with Tracy."

But I didn't want to believe that. I knew why I wanted Brian to be Tracy's murderer. Before Tracy's murder, I'd believed the worst person in town was Tom Gash, who was known for shoplifting in Sky City. He'd been arrested three times. Then Tracy was murdered and I had to face the fact that someone worse, much worse, was probably living in our midst. If Brian, who was probably a child molester, was not Tracy's murderer, then I knew I would never be able to look at anyone in town the same way again.

Who knew what secrets they might have?

I didn't see Jeff at school the next day, so after school I rode my bike over to his house. Everything was quiet. I parked my bike and sat on the wall, wondering if I should go up.

"Charlie." I turned but didn't see him. "Over here." Jeff's voice definitely came from the rose bushes in Mrs. Whitford's garden. I got up and crossed to the gate. "What are you doing in there?" I was hesitant to enter.

"Staying out of sight," Jeff answered. "C'mere."

I went in. I smelled the cigarette smoke before I found him, perched on a mossy rock. "I guess it doesn't matter, " I said. "With Brian in jail and everything."

Jeff gave me a grim look. "He's not in jail."

"What?" I gasped.

"They released him. Marleen claims she was wearing clothes when Brian painted her. She says he never touched her. He says he took a little 'artistic license' with her portraits." He took a drag on the cigarette, then crushed it into the dirt. "She's lying. She does that a lot."

I remembered the first day of third grade when we all introduced ourselves and told where we were from and what we'd done that summer. Marleen stood up and announced she had been to Athens. I'd been reading Greek myths and was totally taken by the soap opera of the gods and goddesses, their loves and wars. We all looked at Marleen as if she were one of those goddesses. "Um, Athens, Georgia, isn't that right, Marleen?" the teacher prodded. Marleen looked a little annoyed, and I had no doubt she'd wanted us to think of Greece. "Of course," she admitted with a roll of her eyes.

Some of that Greek glamour clung to her, though, drawing me to her like a coal miner to a diamond. So her lie had had its desired effect after all.

"So what's going on? Where is she?" I hoped the police hadn't locked her up for lying.

"She's been fighting with Mom and Dad all day. But she wants to see you." Jeff tossed the butt of his cigarette into the damp earth below the rose bushes. "She said you'd know where."

I nodded and started to turn away, but Jeff caught my arm. I looked back and he moved his hand down my arm to hold my hand. "Be careful."

"Why?" I looked around. "Brian's not out here, is he?"

Jeff snorted. "Nah, he wouldn't dare show his face with me and Kyle and Dad all waiting for an opportunity to bash it in. That doesn't mean you're safe out here, though. Just, be careful." He squeezed my hand quickly, then released it and walked back toward his metal building.

I made my way to the clearing on the other side of the rose bushes. The undergrowth had grown back. Brian would soon be weeding and pruning. If he didn't, within a couple of months, the path would be impassable. I broke through the bushes into the clearing.

Marleen lay face down under the rosebushes, her blonde hair spread out over the grass that had just turned green in the past week. Something about the way she sprawled stopped my heart. I thought of red hair spread over brown November grass. "Marleen!" I called, but she didn't answer. Somewhere there were hyacinths blooming because the heady scent filled my nostrils. Terror rose in my throat like a bubble and I opened my mouth to scream…and she rolled over and grinned. "Don't do that!" I yelled.

"Oh, what's the matter with you?" Marleen pouted. "Can't you take a joke anymore?"

"That's not funny." My heart still pumping furiously, I wanted to turn and stomp away, but I stopped. Marleen had a small bruise on her left cheek. I wondered if it was where her father slapped her. "Why are you in such a great mood, anyway? I thought you'd be upset about Brian."

"Why? Now everybody knows we're in love. Of course, he had to tell the police that he had no interest in me, and that he never saw me nude." She leaned toward me and winked. "But that's not necessarily true."

Marleen's giddiness affected me in an odd way. At one and the same time I both wanted to smack some sense into her and hug her. Instead I sat down. "So, what are you going to do?"

"The same thing I've been doing." Marleen shrugged. "Sneak up to his house in the afternoons, pose for him … you know."

Her blasé attitude horrified me, but I knew I had to find another way to get through to her. I grasped at the only straw I could see that might buy me some time. "You don't think you might put him in danger by doing that?"

"What?" Marleen looked surprised.

I thought I'd found a way to save her. "I mean, he might not want you coming up there now. The police are probably watching him."

"What for?" She looked puzzled. "I told them we never did anything. Why would they still be watching him?"

"Tracy." I held up my hands when I saw her straighten her shoulders for a fight. "Well, think about it, Marleen, they're looking for Tracy's murderer. Tracy was a pretty teenage girl. You're a pretty teenage girl and they find naked pictures of you in Brian Whitford's house. They've got to be suspicious."

"Paintings, not pictures." Marleen looked thoughtful. She turned to me a moment later with a canny look on her face. "You did this, didn't you?"

"What?" I felt the same way I did the day when I was six and I got into the candy cupboard and Mom caught me. I knew the guilt showed on my face.

"You turned him in. You called the police and told them to search his house." She was starting to sound angry. "You bitch!"

"I didn't--"

"Then you made Jeff do it. You just couldn't stand that I had a better boyfriend than you, could you?" Marleen's face had turned red.

"I couldn't stand to see you letting some old creep take advantage of you," I shouted. "He's a pedophile, Marleen! You need to stay away from him."

Marleen jerked away from my outstretched hand. "I'll do what I like. I'll marry him if I want to. And you can't stop me!"

She ran then, blind to the bushes and weeds and flowers, tearing through the garden toward the Whitford house. I watched her go, helpless. Then I ran back to her house. Jeff wasn't outside or in the metal building. I ran up to the house and banged on the door. I couldn't have knocked more than twice when it flew open. Marleen's dad, a thick man who reminded me of a mix between a gorilla and a sandbag, stood there in a sleeveless white tee-shirt and blue jeans. I couldn't think of the betrayal anymore. I wasn't betraying Marleen by telling. I was protecting her.

"She's gone, up to Whitfords'," I gasped.

"Christ," was all the gorilla said to me. He turned and yelled over his shoulder. "Kyle, get out here."

Kyle came in from the other room. He looked from me to his father. "What's up, Dad?"

"Your sister's gone back up to the pervert's house. Take your brother and go get her."

Mrs. Galloway came out of the kitchen. Her eyes were bloodshot, but she looked sober. Kyle had already leapt into action. "Jeff!" he yelled, snatching a sweatshirt off the back of a chair. Jeff spoke from behind me. "I heard." He wore a grim expression. "Come on." But before they could move again, there was a knock on the kitchen door. Mrs. Galloway looked around and said, "It's okay, she's here."

I heard murmuring voices, Marleen's shrill cry, "No!" and then thunderous sobs. Then Mrs. Galloway came in, dragging Marleen by the arm. Marleen fell into a chair and began rocking back and forth, holding her arms around her chest and crying. I started forward, but Jeff stopped me. The slight movement caught her attention, however, and she turned, eyes full of hatred on me. "Why are you here?" she screamed. "Haven't you done enough? Get out, get out, I hate you!"

I wasn't sure how Jeff got me out of there because I didn't remember anything after Marleen's screams, but suddenly we were outside, in the spring sun, and he was holding me. "She hates me," I whispered, still shocked from the vitriol in Marleen's voice.

"She doesn't know what's good for her, anymore." Jeff stroked my hair. "Someday she'll realize what a good friend you were to her today."

I tried to draw in a deeper breath, but my lungs wouldn't obey, and I hiccupped instead. "She'll never think that. I'll never talk to her again. I know it." Tears started down my cheeks. "She's my best friend."

Jeff just drew me closer and held me, and I thought about how far he'd come over the past few weeks. If he could open up to me, surely Marleen could remember what it meant to be a friend.

Unfortunately, Mrs. Galloway decided it was time to make a change in their lives. When I went over to her house the next day--Good Friday--I found Kyle's Camaro parked outside with the trunk open. Suitcases were stacked inside.

"They're leaving," Jeff said, and I saw him standing beside the metal building, wiping his greasy hands on a rag. "Mom and Marleen."

"What happened?" I felt as if the air had been sucked from my lungs. I couldn't speak above a whisper.

"After you left yesterday, Mom and Dad got in a huge fight. He was going to slap Marleen again, but Mom stopped him. Then he accused her of teaching Marleen to be a whore. They said some … some pretty awful things to each other. Kyle had to stop Dad hitting Mom. Then Dad stomped out and Mom got on the phone with her sister, the one who lives in Chicago. When she got off, she told Marleen to pack her bags. Then she told me I had to stay here with Kyle since Kyle can't go anywhere as long as he's a suspect."

"So they're moving to Chicago?" I felt numb, as if someone had smacked me. I had never anticipated such an outcome from our anonymous tip to the police. "Where is your dad?"

"Dunno." Jeff tried to sound nonchalant but failed utterly. "He didn't come home last night."

"He didn't come home?" I gaped at him. "Does he even know your mom and Marleen are leaving?"

"Doesn't matter." He shrugged. "It's better this way, you know. Marleen's out of control. If Brian hadn't brought her back yesterday…"

"He brought her back?" I wondered how I'd missed that. I'd realized Marleen had come back unwillingly, but not that Brian had brought her back. "Oh God, how embarrassing for her."

"Yeah, he probably felt he didn't have any choice. The cops are watching him, and he knew if he was seen with Marleen, especially with her in his house, they'd be after him again." Jeff paused, then tossed his rag into the building. "And then there's Dad. He claims she's a lost cause, damaged goods, never be any good to a man again except as a whore. Marleen doesn't need to hear that. Her self esteem is low enough as it is."

"She'll like Chicago." I remembered how arrogant Marleen had acted after Christmas holidays. Part of that had had to do with Brian, of course, but living in Chicago for a week, pretending she belonged there--that had played a big part, too. Maybe she did belong there.

“Yeah, Mom likes it, too,” Jeff said. “And she hasn’t been happy in a while. It’ll be good for her.”

“But what about you?” I looked at him, concerned. “What about Kyle? What if your dad doesn’t come home?”

He shrugged. “He’ll be back. He’s done this before. He always comes back.”

“Won’t he be mad when he finds your mom and Marleen are gone?” I wondered if Mr. Galloway’s fury ever touched Jeff.

“Maybe at first.” He didn’t meet my eyes. “But he’ll be relieved, too. He knows Marleen shouldn’t be here now.”

We sat on the concrete wall. Most of the daffodils were gone, but here and there a jaunty yellow head bounced in the slight breeze. Jeff had a pack of cigarettes in his shirt pocket. I wondered how much he had smoked last night. It occurred to me to wonder where he got the money to buy the cigarettes. I didn’t think his mom and dad would give it to him.

I heard voices and turned to see Marleen, her mom and Kyle coming down the walk. “He’ll be home in a couple of days, at most,” Marleen’s mom said. “Give him the phone number, I’ll talk him around. And if you need anything--“

“We’ll call,” Kyle assured her. “It’s okay, Mom. We’ll be fine.”

He hugged and kissed his mother, then she turned to Jeff. For a moment she hesitated. “It’s okay, Mom.” He stood and smiled at his mother. “Just go.”

She grabbed him and pulled him into an embrace. “I hate leaving you boys.” Her voice hitched. “I always wanted to be there for you.”

I saw Jeff look helplessly at Kyle as they tried to comfort their mother. I turned my attention to Marleen, who stood beside the car with a vacant look on her face. Circumventing the family farewell in front of me, I went to her.

“Marleen,” I whispered. “I’m so sorry. I hope you’ll be happy in Chicago.” I hugged her, but her arms hung limp and unresponsive by her sides.

Then Mrs. Galloway grabbed me and hugged me and when she released me, Marleen was in the Camaro’s backseat, and Kyle was walking around to the driver’s side. He closed the trunk with a thump and glanced at Jeff. “I’ll be back as soon as I drop them off at the bus station. If Dad comes back, stay out of sight until I get here.”

Jeff saluted, then he and I stepped back as the Camaro backed out of the drive. Marleen didn’t look out the window even once as the Camaro drove away. I know, because my eyes never left her window until they were out of sight.

## Chapter Fourteen

"I can't believe she just left those boys with that man!" Mom slapped a pan on the stove.

"He is their father," David sliced an onion and left the slivers on the cutting board while he rinsed the knife. Mom collected them and put them in the pan where they began to sizzle aromatically. "And he's not that bad, sweetheart. He's a foreman down at the quarry, works hard for his family from what I've heard. It can't be easy having three kids."

Mom sighed. "Whatever. From what I've seen, he doesn't show a whole lot of love and support for his three kids."

"I don't think Mrs. Galloway felt like she had a lot of choice," I said. "She wanted to get Marleen away from Brian Whitford." I stopped short of saying "and Mr. Galloway."

"Hmmm." David looked thoughtful. "He's the one we should be focusing on. Or the police should, anyway. I hope they haven't given him up as a suspect in Tracy Collins's murder." He glanced at me. "I guess you won't have much reason to go over to the Galloways since Marleen's gone, but please be careful around Brian Whitford, Charlie. Now that he's lost Marleen, he may be looking for some other innocent girl."

I hesitated in the act of taking down plates. "Well, Jeff and I are still friends," I said. "I might still go see him every now and then." My face burned. Jeff wasn't the type of boyfriend who'd meet me uptown or take me to the movies, so I had to come up with some excuse to go visit him. "You know, make sure he and Kyle are okay."

The moment's silence told me Mom and David were exchanging parental glances behind my back. "Sure, Hon." Mom sounded all casual. "Let me know if they need anything."

"And don't stay late." David's tone was more severe. "I want you home before dark. And when you're there, stay away from the Whitford house. Even if Brian Whitford is just some creepy artist type, I don't want you ending up on one of his canvases."

"Ugh." I turned, wrinkling my nose and trying to hide how relieved I felt.

"Ugh, indeed." Mom added ground beef to the browned onions. It smelled heavenly. David seized me and tickled me until I screamed "uncle" and then he let me go and went upstairs to get Dougie, who'd just woken from his nap.

Saturday was Mom's birthday and all week I debated what to give her. I wanted it to be something special. I had saved up fifty-three dollars from my allowance. I thought of perfume and jewelry and all the other things you get moms you love. Nothing seemed right. On Thursday, I discussed it with Jeff.

He had only one suggestion. "You could give her back your dad's name and address."

We sat on his front porch and a gentle spring rain fell outside. I watched drops of rain splatter and spread on the concrete pad the Galloways used for cookouts--or the one they had used for cookouts in better times.

"What good would that do?" I shifted in the cheap plastic lawn chair. I wondered if it was the same one Marleen had once brought out for me to sit with her outside the Whitford garden.

"It'd show her you trusted her." Jeff handed me a can of soda. "That you believed her when she said getting to know your dad wasn't a good idea."

"Yeah. I guess." I popped the top and thought about his suggestion. Although I had yet to look at the slip of paper in my music box, I knew I wasn't ready to give it up. "What else you got?"

"Perfume, jewelry, the usual." He took a sip of soda and smiled a little. "Remember when all we had to do was make something for our moms and they'd be thrilled? I made my mom a macaroni necklace once and she acted like it was made of pure gold, diamonds and pearls."

"Yeah, I remember." I thought of the lion I'd made my mom out of pipe cleaners when I was five. She still had it in a box in her bureau.

"Maybe you need to think of something like that," Jeff said. "Something sort of sentimental. Moms like that."

I snapped my fingers. "That gives me an idea. But I've got to get to the drugstore today."

He put a hand on my arm. "You can't go anywhere while it's raining."

"Yeah," I settled back into my chair. "I guess not." We were quiet for a while. Jeff took my hand in his and rubbed my fingers. The one thing I had noticed about Jeff was his total inability to be completely still. He liked to be doing something with his hands. His fingers on mine felt nice and I tried to enjoy it, but I was still new to a boyfriend's touch and quickly became uncomfortable with the silence. Then I said, "Have you heard from you mom and Marleen?"

"They're fine." He continued to caress my fingers. "Mom wants me to come up there when school's out. I dunno, though. I might just stay here."

"How about Marleen?" I asked. "Has she started school up there?"

Jeff shook his head. "Mom says she's going to home school Marleen, keep her up on her work, but not put her in school this year."

This year. My heart, which was beating faster than normal anyway, gave an extra little beat. "So they're going to stay? Next school year, too?"

Jeff nodded. He didn't look up, as if he were afraid to catch my eye. "Yeah, I think so."

"What about your dad?" Jeff's dad had taken the news better than any of us had anticipated. After a brief telephone call with his wife, Mr. Galloway had retired to bed. Jeff said his dad had pretty much gotten into a schedule of going to work, coming home late and going straight to bed.

"I think it's pretty much over between them." He released my hand and sat up. "It has been for a while."

I felt sad. How could two people raise three children and suddenly realize they didn't belong together? "Will they get divorced?"

"That'll probably be up to Mom. Dad would go on like this for the rest of his life." He looked outside. The rain slackened. I could feel his restlessness like it was a part of me.

"My mom wanted me to ask if you needed anything." I felt awkward, like I was offering something someone didn't want.

Jeff just shook his head. "We're fine. Dad gives Kyle and me money and we buy what we need for sandwiches and stuff."

"Well, don't be surprised if my mom sends over a casserole someday." I tried to make it sound like a joke. "She doesn't think you can survive on sandwiches alone."

Jeff snorted. "Sure. I wouldn't mind a good meal for a change. But we're not starving. Dad wouldn't let that happen."

I wondered if Jeff's dad was all that great or if Jeff just needed to believe he was. I shrugged it off. "I better go. Mom expects me home by the time it's dark and if I want to do this thing for her birthday, I'll have to get started tonight."

Jeff frowned. "It's gonna be dark soon. I don't like the idea of you out when it's dark."

"I'll be home before it gets too late. Don't worry, Mom would kill me herself if I made her worry too much."

Jeff grinned. "Okay, see you tomorrow." He rose and stretched, bent over, placed his arms on the armrests of my lawnchair, and kissed me. He was so casual about it, it felt great. Maybe that was because he didn't hesitate, as if he didn't have to wonder anymore if I wanted him to kiss me. As if we belonged together and could kiss anytime we wanted. The thought made me happy, and with a lighter heart, I slipped through the remaining drizzle to my bike and pedaled away.

Either it took me longer than I'd anticipated at the drugstore or because of the overcast sky the spring night came much earlier than usual. At any rate, as I pedaled along the street homeward I was very aware that I would not make it before full dark fell. My bike sliced through mud puddles reflecting the streetlamps like big, earthbound moons. Maybe it would be okay, though. Maybe she would be busy with the baby or cooking dinner and wouldn't notice how late it had gotten. I concentrated on pedaling as hard as I could, more afraid of my mother's worry than anything else that might threaten me from the shadows.

My heart sank when I turned into my driveway and saw Mom silhouetted against a block of yellow light that was our front doorway. She held Dougie, who was crying, on her hip.

"Where have you been? I called the Galloways and nobody answered. It's been dark for a good twenty minutes."

I parked my bike in its spot under the eaves, trying to conceal the drugstore bag behind my back. "I just got hung up."

"Hung up?" Mom sounded furious. "Do you have any idea how worried I've been? You do realize there's still a murderer loose out there somewhere, don't you? And you insist on placing yourself under the very noses of two of the suspects."

"Mom--" I understood how upset she was, but I didn't like that she still considered Kyle a suspect.

"Don't interrupt me. This was incredibly irresponsible of you. Charlie!" She seized my arm as I tried to walk past her without letting her see the bag. The bag slipped from my grasp and spilled part of its contents on the floor. I dropped to my knees to gather up the ribbon and birthday card that had fallen out of the bag. "Oh!" Mom froze.

"I had some stuff to do." I straightened with as much dignity as a princess. "Can I go now? I have homework."

Mom looked like she might cry. She set the squirming baby down and he headed for a toy train he'd left in the hall. "You can't just run off like that." Her voice was weak. "I was worried."

"Yeah." I held the bag against me to keep her from seeing anything else. "I got that." I turned and headed upstairs, leaving her standing in the still open door.

Mom's birthday present took longer than I'd anticipated. I was still working on it when she called me down for dinner. She didn't mention the fact that I'd been late. She ladled the ham and bean soup she'd slow-cooked into two bowls, added salad and rolls, and sat. I looked at David's empty spot.

"Where's David?"

Mom took a long time tearing up some roll into bite size pieces for Dougie. "He had to work late." Her voice sounded funny, as if she were trying not to cry.

A fear I'd never anticipated bloomed inside my chest. "Mom?"

She must have heard some of the anxiety in my voice because she looked up and smiled brightly. "It's okay. Really. We had a stupid fight this morning, but we made up and he just had to show a house this evening to some out-of-town buyers. Everything's fine."

I remembered David had already been gone when I got downstairs this morning. "I didn't know you guys had a fight."

Mom shrugged. "We try never to fight in front of you or Dougie."

"You fight?" I couldn't disguise my surprise. "A lot?"

"Every couple fights. We don't fight any more than anybody else." She sighed and spooned a couple of beans onto Dougie's tray. "I guarantee you Cinderella fought with her prince before they even got out of the carriage."

She smiled at me, but the tired look in her eyes didn't reassure me. Still, I wanted to make a joke of the whole thing. "Sure. And the footman probably heard them and told the whole castle about it."

We both laughed, and a moment later David came in, kissed Mom lightly and filled his bowl with soup. I listened to his description of the couple he'd shown the house to while I finished my dinner, then excused myself and went upstairs. Finishing Mom's present meant even more to me now than it had before.

I spent the rest of the evening working on Mom's present. I sorted my materials: glue, scissors, tape, pens, colored paper. I worked steadily until nearly ten o'clock and realized I was done. I examined the gift with satisfaction before going to bed.

Despite Mom's protests the night before and David's apologetic behavior, the two still seemed strained on Friday morning. David lingered longer over breakfast, but Mom seemed determined not to sit down with him. She bustled over coffee and breakfast dishes and the baby's food, letting her own cereal drown itself in the milk. I wondered what had gone on between the two of them before I came downstairs. Again, I felt a twinge of anxiety and confided in Jeff about it after school.

"I wouldn't worry about it." Jeff looked out of the metal building at me. "Every family fights."

"Some fight worse than others." I sat Indian-style on the wall so my legs wouldn't dangle in the weeds.

"I wouldn't think you'd have to worry about being one of those." His voice sounded dry, although his back was to me and I couldn't see his face.

"Maybe not." I nodded agreement. "But Mom and David have never fought like this before. And I don't even know what it's about."

"You don't need to." Jeff moved to the other side of the shed. I heard clinking, metal against metal. "It's between them. You might not want to know, anyway."

"What's that mean?" I didn't like what I thought he was saying.

Jeff moved back into my field of vision. "Just this. Statistically, it's been shown that couples fight about two issues: money and kids. Since your family has plenty of the first, that shouldn't be an issue."

"So they're fighting about me?" I hadn't realized I could be an "issue" for my parents.

He shrugged. "You just might not want to know, that's all."

"But what if--" I broke off, realizing what I was about to say.

"What if he leaves?" Jeff came out, wiping his hands on a rag. His hands left dark streaks of grease on the white cloth. I thought of Brian's small dark handprints on the handles of his garden tools and shivered. He tossed the rag casually back into the metal building. "He loves you. He loves your mom. He won't leave."

I wasn't so sure. "Maybe he loves us, but the baby is the only one related to him by blood. He could leave us. Sometimes love isn't enough."

"Like my mom." Jeff sat beside me, letting his legs dangle in the knee high grass. Jeff was braver than me. "But she left because she loved Marleen, too."

I nodded. I wanted to change the subject, but I didn't want to ask about Marleen. Instead, thinking again of Brian's small hands, I indicated Mrs. Whitford's garden where the snowball bushes had grown enormous blue-white flowers overnight. "Have you seen him recently?"

Jeff frowned at the garden. "He doesn't work in the garden as much since Marleen left. Maybe he's painting."

I raised my eyebrows at him. "Do you think he's an artist for real?"

"Doesn't matter what I think. He's an artist if he thinks he is, regardless of what everybody else in the world thinks." He fiddled with the front pocket of his t-shirt. I knew he was thinking about smoking, trying to resist the impulse to pull out a cigarette.

"Did you see the paintings of Marleen?"

Jeff winced and shook his head. “No. The police took them. Evidence. I guess they’re locked away in an evidence room somewhere.”

“They should destroy them.” I remembered lying out in the sun on Marleen’s deck one summer day before Brian Whitford became an issue. She’d untied her bathing suit top and, holding it up with one hand, she’d asked me to rub some suntan lotion on her neck and shoulders. When I was tying her top back on, my hands slipped and the top fell open revealing her newly budding breasts. Marleen had been shocked, although I’d been stricken by the giggles. Marleen had changed over the months since Brian Whitford, I thought. I wondered how she was doing in her new home. Had she made new friends? Would she ever contact me again? I doubted it. Still, I hated the thought of nude paintings with her face on them existing somewhere.

“At least they’re just paintings,” Jeff said. “Not photos. The police didn’t find any actual evidence that she ever even posed for him.”

I shook my head, knowing the truth. “She told me she had. But I’m willing to bet he asked her.”

“She might have lied.” Jeff sounded hopeful. “Or maybe she posed but not nude.”

“Maybe.” My eyes strayed to the garden again. I wished the police would make an arrest for Tracy’s murder, if only so I could quit worrying about whether or not Brian did it.

"Tomorrow's your mom's birthday, isn't it?" Jeff said, changing the subject. "Your family have plans?"

"I think we're supposed to go out to dinner," I said. "David wants to try the new Italian restaurant."

"What about your mom?" Jeff pulled out the pack of cigarettes. "Where does she want to go?"

I sighed and tried hard not to watch him playing with the cellophane. "I think Mom would prefer to go out alone with David, but she can't find a babysitter she trusts. I told her I'd watch Dougie, but I guess she doesn't trust me either." We were silent for a moment. Then I had to ask. "What makes you think Mom and David are fighting about me?"

Jeff grinned, stuffed the pack into his pocket again and put one arm around me. I leaned into the warmth of him without even thinking about it. "Well, you're a teenager, and not only have you chosen a boyfriend they might not particularly like, he's actually related to a suspected murderer."

"Oh, cut it out." I shoved him, but only a little. "Mom adores you. And Kyle. You guys used to be over at my house all the time."

"Yeah, that was before." Jeff kicked at a brittle yellow weed. A large bug buzzed angrily out, making me jerk away.

The next morning, Mom's birthday, I got up early. I had planned to make breakfast, but David was already there, scrambling eggs. Bacon drained on a paper towel by the stove. Grateful that someone was already doing the manual labor, I sank into a chair and put my head on the breakfast table. I heard the rhythmic scraping of the spatula on the pan as David tossed the eggs back and forth. The microwave dinged. A plate scraped and then landed on the table next to my head. I rolled my head to the side and looked up at David, who smiled. “Thanks for getting up.” The luscious aroma of the cinnamon bun reached my nostrils.

I straightened and took a bite out of the fresh, warm cinnamon bun. I fingered the ribbon on Mom’s present. I’d wrapped it the night before. I watched David as he worked at the stove. He scooped eggs on plates, placed bacon alongside and added buttered toast. I noticed a bud vase on the table with a single red rose in it.

Mom came in. She looked tired. Dougie chortled as he bounced on her hip. She kissed David and smiled a little when she saw the breakfast. David held up a plate of eggs, bacon, toast and a cinnamon roll as if it were an offering of some sort. “Happy birthday.”

“Happy birthday, Mom.” I jumped up and took Dougie from her as I handed her the present. I fastened Dougie into his high chair and gave him a little cinnamon bun to keep him quiet.

“How nice.” Mom smiled, looking around. “You two have been hard at work I see.”

I started to disclaim any credit, but David put his arm around my shoulders. “We were up at the break of dawn.” He winked at me.

Mom sat and examined her gift. “Should I open it now?” She raised her eyebrows at me. When I nodded, she tore the paper and laid the photo album I’d put together in front of her.

“It’s sort of a combination gift for your birthday and your anniversary.” I shot a glance at David as I said it. He wiped his hands on a dishtowel and walked over to stand behind Mom as she opened the album.

The first pictures were of the three of us before the wedding, then pictures of the wedding. On one page, I’d pasted a sonogram of Dougie, framed in blue paper. Mom paused for several seconds here, her fingers caressing the paper. “I didn’t even know you saved this,” she said in a low voice.

“Why not? You’re the one who’s always saying I’m a packrat. I save everything.” As I said it, I remembered the slip of paper I’d saved with my father’s name and address and how Jeff had said I should give it back to Mom. The memory made me pause, but then Mom looked up and her smile was radiant.

“Thank you, Charlie.” She stood and leaned over to hug me, tears in her eyes. “I can’t think of anything I’d rather have.”

After a moment, Dougie began making “mmmm” noises and reaching for the eggs and David laughed. “We’d better feed this child before he implodes.” I noticed his eyes looked bright as he turned away. I hoped this meant my gift had meant something to him as well.

"There's a sidewalk sale today." Mom looked at me. "I thought maybe we could go, Charlie."

I'd hoped to sneak over to see Jeff, but I wouldn't disappoint my mom on her birthday. "Sounds good. I need new jeans."

"I thought you might want a new dress." Mom took a bite of toast. "You know, in case you have a date."

I blushed. "Why would I have a date? I'm too young, aren't I?"

"Yes!" David said, too quickly. "Too young. No dates. I don't need that stress."

Mom and I both laughed.

"Where is the sidewalk sale?" I asked.

"Patton's and the shoe store next door. I could use a new pair of sandals myself." She winked at David.

"It's your birthday, knock yourself out," David smiled. Dougie started making "mm-mmm" sounds again, so David spooned some eggs from his own plate onto Dougie's tray. We all smiled at the baby for a minute, feeling happy and content in our family.

Half of our small town turned out for a sidewalk sale. Patton's was the best department store in town, so when they trotted out the contents of their storage room, the event could possibly make headlines in the local paper. Which meant that Mom and I had to spend some time dressing before we left. Mom French-braided my hair and I watched while she put on lipstick and mascara. Mom never wore much makeup, because she always swore it clogged the pores and made your face look worse. But then, Mom's complexion glowed with health without powder and blush.

It seemed every female in our town over the age of twelve was already browsing the racks of clothing crowded together under the awning outside Patton's. Mothers called to their daughters, What do you think of this? And daughters invariably made faces and turned away.

Mom and I elbowed our way in among the racks of clothing in my size first. I slid past a plump woman to get to the jeans in my size while Mom browsed a rack of frilly blouses. "How about this one?" Several heads turned her way to examine the lacy pink blouse she held up. I noticed some mothers nodding approval.

"Mom, no!" I motioned for her to put it back. "It's too little girly."

Mom shrugged and started to replace the blouse, but another woman reached in. "Sorry." She grinned apologetically. "It should fit my daughter, though."

I hid a smile and bit my lip as I turned away. A rack with denim jackets caught my eye and I edged toward it.

"Hello, Charlie." I jerked in surprise at the male voice practically at my elbow. Brian Whitford, who'd evidently been kneeling on the pavement, stood. He pocketed the quarter he'd picked up. "How are you? It's been a long time."

"Oh, hi, I-I'm fine." I looked around for Mom. She had turned away to speak to a woman she knew. I could only see the woman's gray-frosted red hair from where I stood.

"Have you heard from Marleen?" Brian sidled a little closer to me. "I hope she's enjoying Chicago."

I sucked in a breath. I knew Jeff wouldn't like Brian asking about Marleen and I figured Mr. Galloway would pretty much kill Brian on sight without letting him speak a word. I wasn't sure how to answer, so I looked for an escape. "I have to go. My mom--"

"Oh, she's busy." Brian looked over my shoulder. "What's your rush?" He smiled, edging closer. I looked around again, hoping someone was close enough to see what was happening and put a stop to it. "You never did like me, did you?" He was so close I could feel his breath on me. It smelled bad, like something had soured in his mouth. I backed away as far as I could, racks of heavy denim on both sides of me, the rough brick wall of the store behind me.

"You know, somebody caused Marleen and me a lot of trouble calling the police like that. She seemed to think it was you." He removed a pair of jeans from the rack as he spoke. I noticed his hands had paint on them and his nails were dirty. "It wasn't very nice, ratting on your friends like that."

My mouth had clenched so tightly, my teeth were starting to chatter. I wanted to get out of the racks of clothes, back into the sunlight I could see pouring down on the street. I knew he couldn't do anything there on a street full of people in broad daylight, but even as I thought it, I scanned for an escape route. If he came any closer I decided I'd scream. Any closer at all.

I felt a hand on my shoulder and turned sharply. Mom stood on the other side of the rack, "Charlie, this is Mrs. Collins-- " She stopped, taking in my expression and silence. "What--" But at that moment, all hell broke loose outside Patton's Department Store.

The small red-haired lady who had been standing by my mother's side was suddenly beside me. She must have crawled through the racks to get there so fast. Her eyes blazed as she faced Brian Whitford. "Get away from her! Get away! What are you doing, looking for another little girl to prey on?" Her voice rose into a scream. "Leave us alone, you freak, you monster!" She began to strike out at Brian Whitford who hadn't gathered his wits about him in time to back away from her. He lifted the jeans he still held in front of his face like a shield, but the force of her blows was enough to push him backward.

"I don't--" His voice faded when she shrieked and launched herself at him like a tigress, and then they were rolling past shoppers, past the racks, off the sidewalk and into the gutter.

I caught glimpses of Brian's white face as she slashed at him with her fingernails, opening red rivers, going for his eyes.

I didn't realize I was screaming too until Mom grabbed me and pulled me away. Another woman hurtled past us. "Mom! Mom, stop it!" She grabbed Mrs. Collins's shoulders and managed to pull her partway off Brian, who remained in the gutter. Racks tumbled over as Frieda, our town's only policewoman, came to help. Between the two of them, they forced Mrs. Collins away, and Frieda bent over Brian, pulling her radio from her belt to call for help. But Brian stood, the jeans still clutched in his tiny hands. He scanned all our faces, a look of hatred in his eyes.

"Tiny people." His voice hissed. The blood from the scratches had smeared over his face and mixed with dirt from the gutter. "Tiny town, tiny people, tiny minds. You always have been!" And he threw the jeans aside as if they fettered him to us and stalked away.

"Hey," Frieda yelled, but it was a weak protest at best. She looked from Brian's departing form to Mrs. Collins's wilting one and made her decision. She radioed for an ambulance.

## Chapter Fifteen

Every town has its dark side. An underbelly. The day of the sidewalk sale was the first time I really glimpsed that darkness, but even now I see it as I walk the streets. As an adult, I trace the same path I did that day. Bradford pear trees line the clean, neat streets. The Blue Ridge Mountains stand guard in the background. At the top of Jailhouse Hill, decorative shrubs and a memorial garden surround the prim and proper courthouse.

But I know about the old oak tree in the back. When I think of it, I picture hanging ropes dangling from its branches like Spanish moss. In one of the offices above what's now Gardener's General Store and Antiques, the Ku Klux Klan used to gather before a march. And even without knowing the history of my town, I glimpse the darkness in other ways. I'm a woman now, so I walk the streets with a stranger's eyes and look beyond the gleaming exterior. Behind rickety gates, down alleyways, among the dumpsters. That's where the dark spaces are. That's where the secrets linger.

Mrs. Collins never recovered from her ordeal at the sidewalk sale. Her daughter, who had pulled her off Brian, rode with her in an ambulance to the hospital. This daughter, Tracy Collins's sister, was 26 years old, married and lived in Raleigh. After a week in the hospital, the daughter moved her mother to a "facility" in Raleigh. We never saw her again. After Mrs. Collins left, Mr. Collins continued to live in the brick house with the white columns. He lived almost completely alone, although I heard a few whispers from time to time about women spending the evening with him.

Brian Whitford continued to live in his parents' home. Frieda questioned us all, especially me, about what had happened that day, but she couldn't come up with any reason to arrest him. I had to admit he hadn't actually threatened me, although I had been afraid of him.

After I quit trembling, Mom suggested we go home, but I didn't really want to leave and spoil what remained of my time alone with her. We got so little of it, anyway. I knew she wanted to get some shoes, so we left Patton's and walked down the street to the shoe store. Mom kept her arm around me the whole way. In front of the shoe store, a dazzling array of heels and pumps and sandals of every color decorated two long tables. Mom seemed hesitant to release me, but I felt better. The shoe store didn't have an awning, and the sun shone down on the tables, so a delicious smell of warm leather wafted from the shoes.

"Mom, I'm fine," I put my arm around her waist and squeezed her. "Seriously. Go find your shoes. I'm just going to browse through the sneakers here."

"Okay," Mom squeezed me back and gave me a severe look. "But I'll be right there if you need me, okay?"

"Sure." I shook her arm off and grinned.

"And maybe then we'll go get something to eat?" She raised her eyebrows.

I actually did feel a little hungry. "Yeah, that'd be great. Let's do that."

She moved away and I tried to look at the sneakers. I even picked up a pair, but I kept seeing Mrs. Collins leaping like a ferocious lion at Brian Whitford. I kept hearing Brian's sinister voice hissing at me. For a moment, as I clutched the pair of sneakers to my chest, Brian's voice deafened me, and I clearly saw him rising from the gutter, mud and blood streaked across his face like war paint. Then, as the images dissipated and my anxiety abated, I became aware of voices behind me.

"Did you see it happen?" She spoke in a low voice, obviously disappointed to be so close to the tragedy but not an actual witness.

"I did," another woman replied. "Edna Collins lost it. Went after that guy--Whitford?--that they say murdered her daughter. She was getting the best of him, too, when they broke it up."

A shared laugh. I shuddered. How could they laugh? Didn't they see the lost expression in Mrs. Collins's eyes? Didn't they understand what a horrible thing had happened? And the ugliness in Brian Whitford's face and voice, both before and after the attack. If they had really seen that, could they have laughed?

I walked quickly away, realized I still held the sneakers and set them down on a table with men's dress shoes. I didn't want to accidentally see who the women were. Chances were, I would know them. Their voices sounded familiar. But if I knew them, if I looked at their faces, would I recognize them? Even then, my perception of my hometown had changed. The storefronts looked less shiny and appealing, the people less friendly. And beneath it all I recognized something slimy and unappealing, something I'd never seen before but always knew was there.

Jeff and I sat on the concrete wall behind his metal building. He had his arm around my waist and we'd just finished kissing. He looked up at the sky. "It's going to rain again. C'mon, I've got some work to do."

I followed him into the metal building. We'd been talking about the incident at the sidewalk sale. Jeff hadn't been happy to hear about it, and his concern for me had been what initially started the kissing. However, I liked to think we'd kept at it because it was fun.

The rain started, and I could hear the drops hitting the roof with pings and pops. It felt cozy inside the little building and I could smell the oily, metallic scent I associated with Jeff. I looked around curiously. Toolboxes, old car batteries, cans of motor oil, funnels, and an oddly shaped draped object were pushed back against the walls of the shed. In the center, on a worktable, was a partly rebuilt engine.

"Is that what you do in here?" I asked. "Work on engines?"

Jeff looked at me curiously, then grinned. "What did you think I did?" He shook his head. "Here we've been dating for a couple of months now and you don't know much about me, do you?"

I shrugged and blushed. I couldn't help it. Jeff was right of course. I'd been pretty self-centered. "Why do you do it?"

He shrugged. "Because I like it. And I've started making money off the engines I rebuild. I buy one, rebuild it, sell it and use the money to buy another one and the parts I need. The more I make off an engine, the better the engine I buy can be." He picked up an odd-looking tool and began doing something to the engine. "Listen, about Brian. Was he threatening you?"

I'd hoped we'd finished talking about Brian. "I'm fine. I don't really know what he was doing."

"But it upset you, didn't it?" He seemed tense and angry. "Hand me that socket wrench."

"The whole thing upset me," I located the wrench and handed it over. "It wasn't just Brian. The whole thing was awful. So much hate and anger and then Mrs. Collins just keeled over and I don't know what will happen to her. Mom said she had a nervous breakdown. And then I heard two women laughing about the whole thing. It was just so ugly."

Jeff looked up from tightening a bolt and smiled a little. "I keep forgetting how sheltered you've been all your life. I guess you never have seen it, have you?"

"Seen what?" I shook my head, confused.

"The ugliness. Every town has it. Secrets, lies, hidden anger, feuds. Small towns are the worst, I guess. I mean, I haven't spent much time in Chicago, but the little bit I've been there hasn't really felt that way. See, you've only ever seen the surface of things. You see a preacher shaking the hand of one of his parishioners and you think, how nice. Or two women stop to speak to each other as they drop their kids off at school or run into each other at the grocery store."

"Yeah, so what?" I shrugged. "I've seen all those things a million times."

"So, maybe things are not always what they seem." Jeff stopped working and leaned on the table. "Maybe the preacher is shaking the hand of a pedophile. Maybe the preacher is a closet pedophile and the man provides him with pornography."

"That's really creepy, Jeff." I backed away a step without even realizing what I was doing until my leg came in contact with the cool metal of a toolbox.

"My point is, you can't ever tell for sure what's going on beneath the surface." He returned to work on the engine.

"What about the two women meeting at the supermarket?" I challenged. "Really, I've seen that so often.

They're usually arranging to get their kids together or just gossiping."

"Just gossiping is probably right." He nodded, still working. "They might be talking about somebody else's problems. Maybe the woman who just walked past is having marital problems. Maybe her husband is cheating on her and she doesn't know it. Or maybe they're talking about another family who's getting ready to lose their house. Maybe the husband lost his job and they're going broke. You know how hurtful gossip can be, Charlie; you heard some yesterday, right?"

I remembered the two women laughing about the horrible incident I'd witnessed. I nodded reluctantly.

"Then you are beginning to understand." He set the wrench aside, pulled something off the engine and examined it. "It's always been there, you've just never seen it before."

I was silent for a while. Jeff returned to making his mysterious adjustments to the engine. Then I asked, "What have you seen that's made you so cynical?"

He paused for several seconds, then stopped working on the engine and looked up at me. Just as he was about to reply, a shadow crossed the doorway and I turned. The rain shower was over and the sun had broken out. Steamy clouds rose from the puddles on the pavement. One of the black kids stood just outside the door with a bat and a ball in his hand. "Hey, Jeff Man, you wanna play? Hey, Charlie."

"Hey, Tommy." I waved.

"Later, Tommy." Jeff motioned at his work. "Gotta finish this engine."

"Sure. Gotta pay the bills, right?" With a cheerful wave, Tommy left.

"So?" I prompted when Jeff turned back to the engine.

He looked up. "Are you sure you want to hear this? Seriously, you remember how much yesterday upset you? I could tell you stuff that's much worse than that."

I hesitated. Did I want to know? I wasn't sure. Part of me wanted to retreat to a time before I knew about the darkness. But…

"Tell me," I said. "One thing. That's all I want to know. But I need to hear it, I think."

"Fine." Jeff wiped his hands on a rag and leaned across the engine. His eyes met mine and I held still, barely daring to breathe. "You know Billy Broughton?"

"Sure." I nodded. "I used to be scared of him. The old guy that lives with his mother. He's … simple."

"He's mentally handicapped." Jeff's blatant description made me wince. "You're not scared of him anymore, right?"

"Of course not." I laughed at the thought. "He's really good with bicycles. He fixed the chain on mine once when it came off in front of his house. He showed me how to fix it myself if it happened again."

"Well, Billy used to have a kitten." Jeff looked at me hard. "His mom got it from the humane society. Billy loved that kitten. He carried it around like a baby. You may have noticed he doesn't have it anymore."

I nodded. "I asked him about it once. He said his mom got rid of it."

"She probably did after what happened." He frowned. "I heard Billy yelling one day behind the grocery store. His mom had sent him for milk. He'd brought the cat along just like normal. But there was a group of high school boys hanging out there and I guess they thought it would be fun to torture Billy and his cat. One of them had the cat and had climbed up in a tree. He was pretending he was going to drop the cat. Billy was screaming and running around under the cat. Then something happened. I prefer to think he didn't mean to, but the guy up in the tree let go of the cat. Billy was right underneath it. When the cat fell, it scratched Billy's face pretty bad. But he grabbed hold of it and started running. And the high school boys left, too. None of them ever knew I was there."

I had tears in my eyes at the thought of poor Billy clutching his cat, but I had an awful feeling I hadn't heard the worst yet. My voice quavered as I asked what I didn't want to know. "Did you know them?"

"Yeah." Jeff straightened slowly, as if he had a heavy weight on his shoulders. "I saw them every day."

"Were they friends of Kyle's?" I found it difficult to believe Kyle would keep such company.

He met my eyes. "One of them *was* Kyle."

The shock of his statement had not worn off in time to allow me to either accept or reject it before we became aware of a rise in the noise level outside. "What the hell?" Jeff walked around his workbench and leaned out the door of the metal building. I followed.

It sounded sort of like a rock concert coming down the street. At first, it was just bass, then we started to hear some of the melody and then voices, not singing along, but shrieking, yelling, triumphant. And engines revved and roared. As we stood there, Kyle's Camaro, flanked by a red Corvette and followed by a black Mustang, rounded the corner. The Camaro sped into the drive, spewing gravel, and the Corvette and Mustang followed suit.

Both Jeff and I stared with our mouths open as Kyle hopped out of the car, followed by a blond girl in short shorts. I thought I recognized her as a cheerleader. Tommy Harper, the high school quarterback, hopped out of the Corvette along with a couple more cheerleaders, and some more football players and several girls got out of the Mustang. The guys immediately started doing some sort of victory dance punctuated by war whoops and giving each other high fives while the girls watched with admiration. Then Kyle broke loose and came over to us.

"It's over, little brother. They arrested somebody. Somebody else." He raised his hand as if for a high five.

"Brian Whitford." I stated it.

Kyle gave me a peculiar look. "Hell, no. Some nigger. Mom'll be thrilled, won't she, Jeff? She always said it was a colored boy that did it."

Jeff stared at his brother as if he didn't know him. "Congratulations." His voice sounded choked.

Kyle didn't seem to notice. "Yeah, thanks. Listen, the boys and I have arranged for some entertainment, a little party, you know, up at the house since Dad won't be home for hours."

Jeff shrugged. "You want me to disappear."

"Well, you can come if you want." Kyle glanced at me. "I mean, there's plenty of girls…"

"No thanks." Jeff held up a hand to stop his brother. "Don't worry, I won't disturb you."

"You're the best, Kid." Kyle reached out to ruffle Jeff's hair, but Jeff sidestepped the motion. With folded arms, he watched Kyle lope back over to his friends.

"What about Tracy?" I watched as Kyle slid one arm around the blond and another around a dark, curly-haired girl. I remembered the look in Kyle's eyes right after Tracy was killed. "Do you think he ever really cared about her?"

Jeff sighed. "Yeah, he did. I know he did. It's just that Kyle lives in the moment. He doesn't remember how he felt about Tracy 'cause it isn't part of who he is now. Right now, he's back on top and he's going to live it up."

"Have any of those guys even been around since the whole thing started?" I glared at the boys trailing behind Kyle.

Jeff shook his head. "Wouldn't touch him with a ten-foot-pole yesterday. It was kind of nice. Kyle never had any dates and wasn't invited to any parties, so he was always around. He acted like he cared about Marleen and me, which was something new, you know? Not that he doesn't care, but now he's got his friends back, it'll be hard to tell."

The black kids had resumed their game in the street. One of them hit the ball too hard and it ricocheted off the metal building with a resounding thud. I glanced over, wanting a distraction. "Let's go play ball."

He shook his head. "You should go home."

I glanced up at the lowering sun and realized he was right. Although it was at least an hour away from darkness, Mom would have dinner ready soon. I started to get my bike, but then I turned back.

"You want to come?" I asked. "Mom wouldn't mind. She likes having my friends over for dinner."

"Really?" For a second his face lit up like a little kid's. Then the music started inside, thudding its way into our conversation. The smile faded and he shook his head. "Nah, go on. I better stay and make sure Kyle doesn't get into trouble. If Dad comes home early--" He didn't finish, but I could imagine what he didn't want to say.

"Yeah, right." I hesitated, not wanting to leave him. "Well, g'night."

Jeff put his arms around me and let his forehead rest against mine for a moment. Then he sighed, and I felt his lips brush my hair as he stepped away.

"Night, Charlie." His voice held a note of resignation.

I felt him watching me as I pedaled away, but when I glanced back, he was lighting a cigarette and didn't see.

## Chapter Sixteen

The next morning the front page of the local paper had a huge story about the arrest under the banner headline "Man Arrested in Collins Murder". David silently handed me the paper when I came in. "Looks like they caught him."

"Yeah." I read the first paragraph.

"On Sunday, police arrested Sydney Edward Moore, 35, of 1937 Gray Street, for the murder of Tracy Collins in November. Police state that Moore, who was a handyman for the Collins household, has been under investigation for several months."

I scanned through the rest of the article, which included an account of evidence found in Moore's apartment, to the last paragraph. "A police spokesman stated that Kyle Galloway, boyfriend of Collins and originally considered a suspect in the murder, is no longer under investigation." I pictured Kyle's application to college with that paragraph appended to it. Who would have known that of all his extracurricular activities and awards, this one paragraph would be the most important for his future.

"If only they'd made the arrest a little earlier." Mom sounded sad. I knew she was thinking of Mrs. Collins. We looked at each other and she smiled a little. "I know. Edna was mentally unstable, anyway, but maybe she could have gotten help, avoided such a horrible scene. You know?"

I did know. I was convinced I'd remember the hatred in the faces of Mrs. Galloway and Brian Whitford for a long time. When I woke from vague nightmares from then on, dreams that left lasting but indefinite impressions on me, it was always that day at the sidewalk sale that I remembered.

I handed Mom the newspaper and she perused the story. "I guess Kyle's pretty happy, huh?" She glanced at me.

"Yeah, I guess." I remembered Kyle walking up the steps with his arms around the pretty girls who'd lost faith in him during the investigation. I wasn't young enough not to know what kind of party they'd been planning. I wondered if Jeff had gone in, but I knew he probably hadn't. Maybe he'd spent the night on the hood of Kyle's Camaro looking up at the stars. More likely, he'd huddled inside the Camaro until the music got quiet and then snuck in.

"I invited Jeff to have dinner with us." I wasn't sure why I said it, but it seemed important.

Mom folded the paper and looked at me with raised eyebrows. I didn't dare look at David, afraid I would blush, but I made myself meet my mother's gaze. "He didn't want to come?" she said after several seconds.

"Well, I guess there was a kind of family thing going on last night." I looked away.

"Okay." Mom nodded. "But next time, don't let him say no. I kind of miss Jeff. You two used to be such good friends. I remember when you had your falling out."

"Our falling out?" I remembered playing with Jeff as a kid in only a very cloudy sort of way. I certainly didn't remember a time when we'd fought.

Mom smiled at her memory. "Oh yes. There was another little girl in the neighborhood, Bridget, who liked Jeff. She was closer to his age, I think. You were only about six or seven. You and Jeff had been inseparable since you were only about three. I think you liked him better than Marleen. Anyway, Bridget came over to play one day with the three of you. I don't know what she said, but suddenly you just stood up and told Jeff he'd have to choose her or you. Well, maybe Jeff was taken in by her curls and green eyes or maybe he just didn't like you giving him an ultimatum. At any rate, he chose Bridget and the two of them went off to play on one side of the yard. Well, you just tossed your little head and went over to play with Marleen on the other side. I thought I would die. I couldn't decide whether to laugh or cry."

For a moment, I wasn't sure, either. Had I become best friends with Marleen to spite Jeff or had she been my consolation prize? "What happened to Bridget?" I couldn't remember a little girl of that name in school.

"She moved away six months later. But Jeff stopped coming to visit after that. What's he doing now, anyway?"

"He rebuilds engines, for one thing," David said. When Mom and I looked at him, he shrugged. "What? I checked him out when you started hanging out with him. A dad's gotta look out for his girl. Anyway, he's got a good reputation. A few men in town have bought his engines and think pretty highly of him as a businessman."

I hadn't realized David and Mom knew how much I was hanging out with Jeff. It sort of made me feel good to know they were paying attention.

The school hallways buzzed with the news about the arrest. Dominique Grady stopped me in the hall after Social Studies. Everybody figured Dominique would be the head cheerleader for the junior varsity football team next year when we started high school. I'd hardly ever spoken with her.

"Great news about Kyle." She patted me on the shoulder as if it were a victory for me, too. "I'm sure Jeff is ecstatic. By the way, do you think Marleen will be back now?"

"I don't know." I wondered why she cared. Marleen was cute, but she'd never cheered as far as I knew. But maybe that didn't matter. Maybe Dominique was afraid Marleen would decide she wanted to cheer next year. You didn't have to have experience to be on the squad, just know the cheers.

"Well, if you hear from her, tell her we all miss her," Dominique said with a sugary smile. "I was hoping she'd decide to cheer next year. We'd talked about it, you know."

No, I didn't, but I didn't care to let Dominique know that. As she walked away, I wondered why it hadn't occurred to me before that Marleen might have grown away from me in more ways than one. Perhaps Brian Whitford hadn't been our only obstacle.

Deep in thought about Brian and Marleen, I bypassed Jeff's metal building and slipped into Mrs. Whitford's garden that afternoon. I wanted a few minutes to think. Everything had turned green, in keeping with the season. I remembered Marleen lying on the pale green grass when there was still a slight chill in the air. School would be over soon. I'd spent more of this year without my best friend than I had with her.

I found our little clearing, which had been overtaken by weeds in just the past couple of weeks, and sat on a small stone. Lost in thought, I started when I realized I wasn't alone in the garden.

Cigarette smoke wafted to my nostrils, competing with the smell of damp earth and lavender. I turned and then shrank back into the budding rose bushes when I spotted Brian Whitford. He wasn't working, just wandering the garden with his hands in his pockets. Paint spatters stained his clothing, and they looked like they hadn't been washed in a while. I snuck a look out at him and saw a spade, shovel and pair of clippers leaning against the back wall of the house, outlined in their own shadows. I looked back at Brian, standing about four feet away from me. I hadn't seen him since the sidewalk sale. I couldn't tell if the scratches on his face had healed or not because a scruffy beard covered his jaw, growing like the weeds in his garden. What would I do if he spotted me? The smartest thing would probably be to run. But if I ran, I'd be admitting I was afraid of him.

Brian didn't look at me. He stood for a long time, smoking and looking into the distance. I hardly dared to breathe. Then he bent, plucked a tiny green weed from the overgrown path, examined it and flung it away. He smiled, his teeth yellow against the bleached paper of the cigarette, and walked back to the gate and out of the garden.

"He knew I was there," I told Jeff later in the metal building.

He frowned at me. "That was pretty dumb, going in there."

"Yeah, I know. I was just thinking about Marleen." Something occurred to me and I looked at him. "Did you know we were friends--you and me, that is--before Marleen and me?"

"Yeah." He grinned a little sheepishly. "Don't you remember? You told me I'd have to choose who I wanted to marry. You or some other girl. I don't even remember her name. But I chose her because you irritated me talking about getting married."

I screwed up my nose. "I sound like a little nit."

"Sorry." His grin widened.

"No, I sounded that way when my mom told me the story, too." I sighed. "She said to tell you she misses you."

He gave me a teasing look. "Your mom was always so cool. Now, if *she* had asked me to marry her, I might have done it."

"Ah!" I pretended to be offended. "Well, you can't now, so there. She's already happily married. But she did say that the next time I ask you to dinner, I shouldn't take no for an answer."

"Are you asking?" Jeff raised his eyebrows.

"I'll let you know." I folded my arms across my chest and glared at him. "What happened last night?"

"What you'd expect." Jeff shrugged and returned to polishing the engine he'd been working on. It looked shiny and almost new. "Kyle and his friends partied until Dad came home and made them stop, then they all woke up with hangovers this morning."

"Your dad wasn't mad?" The thought of Mr. Galloway angry still made me cringe.

"He was too happy for Kyle." Jeff looked at me curiously. "He's not a bad guy, you know. He just works hard and expects people to accommodate him when he's at home."

I heard cheerful whistling and looked out the door to see Kyle practically skipping down the steps. It seemed wrong, like singing at a funeral. I noticed a black kid walking past, tossing a ball in the air and catching it in a mitt with a thwack. The sound of the baseball hitting the glove had an ominous note, or maybe it was the way the kid eyed Kyle with animosity.

"Look out!" I yelled before I realized I'd seen the black kid draw his arm back. Kyle turned and ducked as the baseball sped past his head and smashed into the side window of the Camaro, sending cracks skittering across the glass. The kid yelled something and took off.

"Hey!" Kyle shouted and ran after him. Jeff brushed past me and followed his brother. I stood frozen for a moment, then walked over to where the baseball had ricocheted off the glass to land in the green grass. It looked deceptively peaceful in the grass. But when I got closer, I saw the angry black markings on the ball. Someone had written "LIAR" boldly across the top. There were other words, but before I could turn the ball over to read them, I heard voices and looked up. Kyle and Jeff marched up the road, talking excitedly.

"Oh man, would you look at this?" Kyle ran his hand over the spiderweb pattern in his window.

Jeff grimaced, and I knew it hurt him to see the Camaro marred in any way. "I can fix it. Maybe now you're working again, you can get the glass on credit."

"Yeah, I'll stop by and see today," Kyle said as I cleared my throat.

"What's up?" Jeff turned to me immediately.

I pointed to the ball with my toe. His brow furrowed, Kyle picked the baseball up. As he did, I saw the word "MURDERER", even bolder than the word "LIAR". It looked like the words had been written in magic marker and "MURDERER" stood out because it had been gone over three or four times. Kyle turned the ball in his hand, then handed it to Jeff. "I've got to get to work."

I put out a hand to stop him. "Don't you think we should call the police?"

Kyle shook his head. "I don't need any more publicity. I just want to be left out of it."

"She's right, Kyle." Jeff looked at the creeping lines of broken glass. "We should call the police. Something like this--it could get real ugly."

"My whole life has been as ugly as it'll ever be these past few months." Kyle strode to the driver's side of the car. "I'll call the auto glass place from work, see if they'll float me some credit."

Jeff stood with the ball in his hand as his brother drove away. I touched his arm. "What does it mean?" I pointed at the ball.

He shrugged. "It means somebody, probably a lot of somebodies, still thinks Kyle murdered Tracy. From the looks of it, they're not real happy the murder was pinned on a man they think is innocent."

I looked up at the Whitford house and at the same moment, Jeff threw the ball as hard as he could into the Whitford garden. I watched it disappear beneath the sun-drenched rosebushes. I imagined I saw something skitter away from the impact.

## Chapter Seventeen

Kyle continued to receive hate messages over the next few weeks. They weren't as violent in action as the baseball, but the words shocked me with their twisted anger. Some of the messages came in the form of anonymous hate mail. Jeff said one arrived with nearly every mail delivery, in fact. The Galloways also received plenty of prank calls and woke one morning to find the yard a ghostly world of toilet paper.

"Doesn't it seem like at least some of these people would've come out of the woodwork when I was actually considered a suspect?" Kyle asked as he maneuvered his Camaro into its new parking spot near the front door. Kyle had started parking his car there for fear vandals would scratch the paint, break the windows (including the new one Jeff had installed), or flatten the tires.

Jeff motioned his brother to pull forward a little. "Okay, there." He leaned on the car door for a minute, talking through the open driver's window. "It's not that they're so convinced you did it, you know."

Kyle cut the engine. "What do you mean?"

Jeff shrugged and pushed off the side of the car."They want a scapegoat, somebody else to blame it on." He sat back down next to me on the root of the oak tree and put his arm around my waist. "They don't want it to be Sydney Moore."

"You mean the niggers." Kyle got out and leaned against his car. His eyes were narrowed and he looked angry. He was angry a lot. Funny how I'd never imagined him angry just a few short months ago. But everything had been different then. I leaned my head on Jeff's shoulder.

Jeff gave me a squeeze and took my soda can out of my hand. "I mean the black community." He took a sip. "They don't think he did it, and since you were the last suspect before him, they've chosen you as the scapegoat. And this kind of violence will only get worse. It won't go away until there's some sort of resolution."

Kyle sighed and shifted from one foot to the other. "You think I should go to the cops."

Jeff shook his head. "Oh hell no. Who are they going to arrest? Half the town? No, you were right. Keep your head down, go about your business. Eventually, the anger and hate will shift its focus, probably about the time Moore goes on trial."

Kyle brightened, as if his brother had solved all his problems. "That's next week. And when did you become such an expert in human relations, little brother? I thought if it didn't have an engine, you didn't know how to work it."

"I'm full of surprises." He handed me back my soda.

"Well, let me treat you to a burger for dinner, then. You can enlighten me on the solutions to race relations."

"He can't," I said, even as Jeff opened his mouth to accept.

"Why not?" Jeff pulled away a little and looked at me.

"Because you're coming to dinner at my house." My cheeks burned. "Mom's fixing spaghetti and meatballs."

Kyle snorted. "Well, can't pass that up, can you? It's fine, little brother. Maybe tomorrow."

After he left, Jeff turned to me. "Did your mom really ask you to invite me again?"

"Yes, this morning." I took a deep breath, willing the embarrassment to alleviate, even as I avoided his gaze. "Do you think Kyle really would have taken you out for that burger?"

Jeff smirked. "Nah, by the time dinner rolled around, he'd've forgotten all about it."

"So I'll see you tonight." I finally let myself look directly at him.

"Looks like." He kissed my nose, smiling right at me in a way that didn't embarrass me at all.

I went home early to help Mom with dinner. Just as I was mixing the salad greens and enjoying the aroma of diced Vidalia onion and garlic bread, I heard a soft putt, putt outside. Mom slid the garlic bread into the oven. She didn't seem to have noticed anything, so I hopped off my stool and went to investigate.

I opened the front door just as Jeff reached for the doorbell. "Hey." I looked at the bunch of flowers he held against his freshly ironed white shirt. "Are those for me?"

"Nope." He smiled. "Your mom."

"How sweet." Mom walked up behind me and took the flowers Jeff held out to her. "It's wonderful to see you again, Jeff." She gave him a motherly kiss on the forehead. I smirked, but Jeff didn't seem to mind at all. "You're much taller than the last time I saw you."

"It's good to see you again, too, Mrs. Bennett," he said.

Mom smiled and left to put the flowers in water. Jeff grabbed my hand. "C'mere." He jerked his head at the door. "I want to show you something."

He drew me over to the side of the porch and I saw the little scooter leaning on its kickstand next to the garage. "What is that, a moped?" I followed him outside, looking at the scooter curiously.

"It's a 1954 Vespa scooter," Jeff said. "I got it off this German guy a couple of years ago. Didn't work at all then, and the parts are hard as hell to come by, but I got 'em."

"Cool." I ran my hand along the smooth lines of the scooter, recognizing it as the covered shape in the metal building. For the first time, I understood Jeff's drive to fix things. It was a cute, sleek little thing, and I had a sudden desire to be on the back of it, with or without Jeff, feeling the wind in my hair and the sun on my face.

"It's not a motorcycle, so I don't have to have a license to drive it." Jeff grinned at me. "Be nice to me and maybe I'll take you for a ride on it sometime."

That reminded me. "Oh, by the way, don't be surprised if my parents ask you all sorts of questions about yourself. David and Mom have this idea that we're like, you know, dating."

"Oh." Jeff was silent for a minute. "Well, we aren't exactly dating, are we? I've never taken you out anywhere."

"I don't expect you to." I spoke in a rush, eager to prove I was no more involved than he was. "I mean, we're just--"

He broke me off with a kiss as he put an arm around my waist. "You're just my girl." His words warmed me, and he stepped back, reaching into his pocket and removing a small box. He kissed me again as he put the box into my hands. "I got you something. It's only fair, you helped with that last engine restoration."

"You've got to be kidding. I don't know the difference between a piston and a block." I felt a little pride that I knew enough to use those words, though.

Jeff grinned, still holding me. "Open it."

Somehow, even with his arms around my waist, I managed to open the tiny white box. Inside was a small silver charm in the shape of a Camaro on a slender silver chain. He let me go long enough to take the necklace from the box and fasten it around my neck. "So you won't forget you're my girl."

I looked up at Jeff and smiled. "Thank you," I said. I wanted to say more. I wanted him to know how much his friendship meant to me. I wanted to somehow put into words the way his arms around me felt. Mostly, I wanted to kiss him, so I did.

At that moment headlights washed over us and I looked around to see David's car pulling into the driveway. He scowled at us from behind the windshield before he pulled his car into the garage. I had no doubt he'd seen us, and I groaned.

"Oh crap, that's just going to make him that much worse!"

Jeff chuckled, released my waist and took my hand as we ran inside.

Dinner went better than I'd expected. David didn't mention seeing us outside, although he did ask Jeff about the Vespa. He and Jeff chatted easily about Jeff's engine restorations. I hadn't known David knew so much about cars. Mom winked at me when they got excited about something called a "283 engine with ram-jet fuel injection system", which had evidently been introduced for the first time in the 1957 Corvette.

When dinner was over, David asked Jeff to show him the Vespa, and I helped Mom with the dishes.

"David likes him." Mom elbowed me in the ribs.

I grinned, rinsing a glass and placing it in the drainer. "You think?"

"Yeah, that's pretty good, huh?" Mom grinned teasingly. "I remember my father hated my first boyfriends."

"Yeah." I looked out the window. I could see David and Jeff examining the scooter. "Pretty good."

When we finished with the dishes, I went outside and listened as David and Jeff discussed the future of scooters like Mopeds and Vespas on America's highways. Then Mom called to David to come help her with something vague enough so I knew she was just giving me some time alone with Jeff before he had to leave.

"Thanks for inviting me," Jeff said as we sat on the front steps.

"It won't be the last time." I knew if Mom had anything to do with it, Jeff would be a frequent guest.

He took my hand. "Even if it is, I'll remember it. Even if we never sit here like this again, I'll remember what it felt like to be part of a real family for once."

He touched the silver Camaro charm as it nestled in the hollow of my neck. "Looks good there," he said with an air of satisfaction.

I leaned my head on his shoulder and we sat that way for a while watching the stars come out one by one. Then Jeff got back on the Vespa and started the motor. I watched the red taillight disappear around the corner.

I went back inside, pausing in the living room where David and Mom were watching television. David looked up and nodded. “He’s a good kid.” I knew I could stay with them, but I went upstairs. I wanted to lie on my bed and think about how the wind would feel in my hair as I perched on the back of Jeff’s Vespa.

The phone rang at six thirty the next morning. I groaned and rolled over. No fair being woken up so early on a Saturday. I heard David’s voice on the phone, muffled. He talked for several minutes, his voice low and somehow ominous, like the first growls of thunder. I rolled over onto my back. Silence fell, a humid shadow over the house. Then I heard Mom’s voice, a flicker of lightning. With my eyes closed so I couldn’t see the bright sunlight that snuck past my shades, I felt a thunderstorm approaching. Then Mom cried “No!”, the lightning struck and I sat up, wide awake. Something awful had happened.

Darkness in the hallway, the sounds of Mom sobbing, the stale smell of last night’s spaghetti and meatballs. I knocked softly and opened their door without waiting for permission. David held Mom against his shoulder and when he saw me, he held out his hand.

“Who died?” I didn’t mean to sound callous, but I knew from Mom’s reaction that death was the shadow I felt hovering over the house. David shook his head, turning away, and it was

Mom who stood, crossing the room to me. I bit my lip, knowing from their actions the death would affect me. I fought against a rush of dread. "What happened? Who was that on the phone?"

Mom pushed my hair back over my shoulders, taking a deep breath. I noticed the shiny trails of her tears tracing the outline of her nose. "It was Kyle, sweetie. There was an accident. Jeff…"

"No, Jeff's fine. He was here for dinner last night, remember?" He called me his girl, he put his arm around me and kissed me. He couldn't be… I touched the silver necklace I'd worn to bed.

David spoke then. His voice sounded empty. "Jeff was in an accident on his way home, Charlie. It was a hit and run. They found him early this morning."

Something inside me dropped, down, through my stomach, my bowels, my feet, the floor, perhaps ending up downstairs somewhere, perhaps going on for eternity into hell. "No." I rejected what he said. "No, he's fine. He can't be…"

"There was nothing they could do." My mother's voice sounded like brittle glass. "Kyle's pretty broken up."

"Yeah, I bet." I remembered Kyle walking away with a girl on each arm, prepared to party the night Tracy's murderer was arrested. I felt whatever had fallen out of me resurging, and I knew I was going to throw up. I stumbled into the bathroom, fell to the floor and clutched the porcelain bowl until my stomach was as empty as my heart.

Mom followed me, supported me and placed a cool washcloth against my forehead, but when she moved to stroke my hair, I pulled away. My throat and eyes and face were all hot, but the rest of me was ice cold. I didn't want her to feel that.

"Where are you going?" She sounded alarmed.

"To bed." I choked on the words and brushed past David, who stood at the door. "It's Saturday."

I sensed movement arrested behind me, as if Mom had started after me but David had grabbed her arm to stop her. I was glad he hadn't allowed her to follow me. I needed to be alone.

I sat in front of my dressing table staring at the music box for so long I memorized the pattern on top. Pink ribbon swirling around pink and yellow roses. The paper cover had worn down on the corners, revealing small scabs of gray cardboard. Every now and then, a tear would slide down my cheek and splatter on the paper-covered cardboard, but I'd wipe it away, my fingers caressing the box. It would take only a second to find out what my father's name was. Just open the lid and the envelope. I touched the silver Camaro charm I still wore around my neck. I remembered Jeff telling me to throw the paper away. "None of your business anymore," he'd said.

After a while, I heard Mom and David go downstairs. I smelled eggs and bacon cooking, heard them talking in low voices and knew I didn't want to see them but I had to get out.

My window wasn't low enough to the ground to jump out. The builder had not provided a convenient trellis. However, Mom and David were in the kitchen at the back of the house. If I was quiet, I could get out the front.

Outside, I realized my bike was locked inside the garage, so I started walking. I walked a long time, concentrating on each step, until I saw a police car parked sideways in the road ahead. A few people had gathered beyond some yellow tape. As I got closer, I saw policemen guarding the tape. Someone lifted the twisted remains of a Vespa onto the back of a tow truck. I skirted the area, walking through the dewy grass on the other side of the road and letting the soft and prickly fir branches brush against my face and hair.

I walked on, reached the dark, silent Galloway house. Kyle's Camaro wasn't there. Was he still at the hospital? Had he gone to the funeral home? What happened when somebody died? I didn't know. Was Mr. Galloway with him? I hoped so. I wanted to think Jeff meant more to them than they'd ever let on.

I slid the metal door of Jeff's building aside. I wondered why he'd never bothered locking it. Didn't he know what kind of world we lived in? He'd called me an innocent, but in the end, it was Jeff who'd fallen victim to the world's wickedness.

The engine he'd just finished rebuilding gleamed in the morning sunlight. What kind of engine was it? What kind of car did it power? I'd never bothered to ask. I sank down to the stained concrete floor and thought about all the things I'd never bothered to ask Jeff. My fingers twined in the silver chain around my neck and I watched as the block of sunlight from the open door moved across my feet, trying to warm me as I huddled in the cold shadows and gave myself up to my grief.

I was still crying when Kyle and his dad came home but by the time David came to get me, the tears had stopped,

Marleen and her mother came home for Jeff's funeral, which was scheduled for Wednesday afternoon. Mom had let me stay home from school all week, and she went with me to Jeff's funeral. I was surprised that I wasn't the only one from school to show up for the funeral. Family, friends and a lot of kids I recognized filled the church. It made me happy that so many people had come to say good-bye to Jeff.

I saw Marleen sitting next to her mother, dressed all in black with her hands in her lap. She looked like a model daughter, a perfect young girl. Mrs. Galloway leaned on her husband, and Kyle sat next to Marleen, his back straight, his eyes fixed straight ahead.

Throughout the service, I kept remembering the sound of the dirt falling on the dead squirrel. I couldn't imagine what hearing the sound of dirt hitting the top of Jeff's coffin would be like. As Mom and I got into the car after the service and she prepared to follow the caravan to the graveside, I stopped her. "Don't."

The only word that I could summon was enough for her. After everyone else had gone, Mom and I went home. I kept imagining the graveside services. I could see Marleen and Mrs. Galloway standing by the grave dressed in black, Kyle and Mr. Galloway slightly behind them. The minister standing at the head of the grave. A polished coffin, freshly offloaded from the hearse. Brass handles. A sharply delineated rectangular hole in the ground. A hole they'd lower Jeff into. How did they do that? I suddenly wished I'd gone. I would have gone if I hadn't dreaded the sound of the dirt hitting the top of the coffin. They'd do that. The preacher would talk and then Mrs. Galloway and Marleen would lay a rose on top of Jeff's coffin and then they'd lower the coffin somehow and then Mrs. Galloway and Marleen and Kyle and Mr. Galloway would file past and drop a handful of red clay into the hole. And it would echo loudly as it hit the coffin lid. A sound that meant he was gone and they'd accepted it.

I remembered the squirrel's funeral and how I'd thrown the handful of dirt into the tiny grave Jeff had dug. I giggled and covered my face with my handkerchief, choking on wild laughter while tears ran down my face and my mother squeezed my hand, thinking I was crying.

At home, I changed clothes and rode my bike over to the Galloway house. Cars were parked up and down the block, so I knew the funeral was over and everyone had come back to eat and drink at the Galloway house. I leaned my bike against the metal building and noticed there was a padlock on it now. I wondered if the engine was still in there.

"Dad put that on," Marleen said, coming down the steps. She wore her funeral dress. "He said he was worried about vandals. Kyle's still getting a lot of hate mail."

"Doesn't the trial start soon?" I tried to sound normal, as if we hadn't been apart for so long a lifetime might have passed.

"Tomorrow." Marleen sat on the concrete wall and smoothed her skirt over her legs. "Kyle blames himself, you know."

"What?" I frowned. "What for?"

"Jeff," Marleen said. "He thinks Jeff was killed by somebody who thinks Moore is innocent."

"Why?" I sat next to Marleen. Unconsciously, I mimicked her actions and smoothed my jeans against my legs.

"The police found skid marks next to where Jeff was found. They say it looks like somebody ran him off the road on purpose."

"Oh my God." My heart felt like it had gotten stuck in mid-beat. In that moment, I realized how hate feeds off itself. "Kyle's not … not going to do anything about it, is he?" I dreaded her reply.

"Who knows?" She might as well have said "Who cares?" "Kyle's such an idiot, he might do anything." Her eyes wandered up toward the Whitford house, and I knew nothing had changed. She still didn't care about anything but Brian Whitford.

"How long are you home for?" I hoped it wouldn't be long.

"Dunno." Marleen shrugged. "Mom didn't say. She's got a job in Chicago now, though, so we'll probably be heading back soon." She sighed. "I guess you kind of miss Jeff, huh?"

I didn't look at her. The question sounded so callous and offhand, I wasn't sure how to react, but the words brought a lump into my throat.

"You guys were sort of dating, weren't you?" She looked at me with a kind of overt curiosity that turned my stomach.

"Yeah." I hesitated. Marleen's attitude didn't invite confidences, but I wanted to talk to somebody. I felt if I didn't talk to somebody, something inside me would implode and leave nothing but darkness in its place. "Sort of. I mean we hung out together, but we hadn't ever actually gone anywhere together."

"Did he kiss you?" She stretched her legs out in front of her and examined her shiny black leather shoes.

With a shock that coursed through my body to my very bones, I remembered that first kiss. I closed my eyes. "You don't need this," Jeff said, crushing out his cigarette. I opened my eyes and looked at Marleen.

She must have seen the pain in my eyes because she grinned suddenly and stood up. "Good. I hoped he had. Now you know how I felt when you took Brian away from me."

The cruelty of her words stunned me enough to keep me frozen to the wall long after she tripped lightly up the steps and back to the funeral party.

## Chapter Eighteen

On Thursday, the trial of Sydney Moore started. Perched on the back of one of the benches lining Main Street, I watched police lead him from the courthouse. Media and crowds of people, black and white, milled in front of the courthouse, contained only by yellow police tape and four uniformed officers. Guards led Sydney Moore in shackles from the courthouse to a waiting police car among flashes of light and a roar from the gathered crowd. White women, women I'd seen in church on Sundays, shouted accusations at him while black women cried out their support in oddly similar voices. Sydney Moore seemed more confused than anything else by the ruckus. He ducked his head, a glazed look on his face, and I thought he'd probably retreated somewhere else in his brain.

"Hey, Charlie." I looked down to see Tommy, his brown features solemn for once.

"Hey, Tommy." I slid off the back of the bench. "What's up?"

"I just wanted to tell you I'm sorry about what happened to Jeff." Tommy kicked the back of the bench, looking frustrated and defensive at the same time. "It wasn't right, what happened to him. Jeff's about the only white boy that's ever been friendly to us."

"Yeah." I felt a now familiar pang in my heart. "He was pretty special."

Tommy nodded and moved away. Marleen replaced him almost instantly. "Whatcha doing, Charlie? Chumming up with my brother's murderer?"

"Tommy never hurt anybody, Marleen." I started to walk away. After what Marleen had said to me after Jeff's funeral, I had no desire to talk to her.

"Maybe not him, but I bet one of his buddies did," Marleen said from behind me. "That's what the cops think, anyway."

I laughed. "The cops think one of Tommy Smith's friends killed Jeff? That's ridiculous. Best I know, none of Tommy's friends even own a car."

"You know what I mean." Marleen's face twisted into an angry snarl. "The cops think it was some black. Because of Kyle."

"Well, Tommy had nothing to do with it." I marched away, wishing she'd leave me alone. I didn't like the way she clumped all black people together. It was too "us" and "them" for me.

But Marleen seemed intent on walking the whole way home with me. As we passed the library, she grinned. "You know, Mom's thinking about staying. She and Dad have patched things up some. And I've promised to be a good little girl. Stay away from that nasty Brian Whitford and all."

I looked at her. I didn't believe her for a second. If Brian Whitford was dumb enough to let her in his front door again, she'd go willingly. "You should do that. If you don't, you could ruin your life and his."

She sniffed. "Only because my parents are narrow-minded fools. But don't worry about us, Charlie. We've learned our lesson."

"Right." I shrugged. "Well, I've seen how far worrying about you will get me, Marleen, so I won't be losing any sleep." I made a sharp left turn into the library and left her standing on the sidewalk smirking after me.

The trial continued the rest of the week and the next. I avoided downtown, but I still heard about the scuffles that took place between white and black. The police guard was doubled to protect Sydney Moore and they stopped taking him out the front door of the courthouse when someone threw a bottle at him. The bottle exploded at Moore's feet, sending shards of green glass outward like deadly dandelion fluff.

School ended, leaving me with even more time on my hands. Or at least that's the way I imagined it. I read about the trial and the racial tension that had taken over my town in the newspaper. Sometimes I imagined Jeff standing over my shoulder as I read. He'd be nodding knowingly since he'd predicted the whole thing. Sometimes when I read about the trial,

I felt a pain in my fingers and looked down to find them tangled in the silver chain and the Camaro charm that I still hadn't taken off.

I rode my bike a lot. I avoided passing the Galloway house because I didn't want to run into Marleen. I wondered sometimes if she'd started going back to Brian's yet, but I had no way of knowing. Maybe that was why I made the turn onto her street without thinking one day in late June. I paused outside her house, looking up at the expressionless windows. Nothing to see here, they told me. I didn't believe them, though, especially when Kyle slammed out of the front door and bounded down the front steps.

"Charlie, have you seen Marleen?" he called. I noticed he'd gotten a haircut. A bee buzzed past his ear and he swatted at it.

"Nope." Without meaning to, I glanced up at the Whitford house.

Kyle followed my glance. "Yeah, I thought of that, too. But I don't think Brian'd let her in, even if she went up there, do you? He got pretty scared last time."

I remembered how Brian had returned Marleen to her family within minutes of her last venture to his house. I shrugged. "Maybe, maybe not."

"You're right, I'll check." Kyle turned, then hesitated and looked back. "We've missed you, Charlie. You're the best friend either my brother or sister have ever had. I know Marleen's pretty thorny right now, and I don't blame you for not hanging out with her. But you could come by and see Mom sometime, you know."

"Sure." I remembered Mrs. Galloway passed out on the couch with the booze in one hand and the burning cigarette in the other. Now that Jeff was gone, I was torn between anger, pity and disgust when I thought of Marleen's mother. If she hadn't left, maybe Jeff would still be alive. If she'd taken him with her, he definitely would be.

"Right." Kyle nodded, and I saw more understanding in his eyes than I'd expected. "I'm going to go check up at Whitford's now. See you around."

I watched him stride up to the house and around the corner, skirting the garden. I had just placed my right foot on the pedal, preparing to get underway when the back gate to the garden opened and Marleen spilled out. She had leaves in her hair and dirt on her face. I gaped in surprise. "What happened to you?"

Marleen gave me a superior look. "Love." She straightened her clothing. "It won't be denied. Brian and I are star-crossed lovers like Romeo and Juliet, but we don't care."

"You do realize Romeo and Juliet died, don't you?" I asked. "Star-crossed lovers are not allowed to be together. Hence the term 'star-crossed.'" I paused, thinking of Jeff.

Marleen rolled her eyes. "If I were to listen to you, you'd really get me down, Charlie."

"If you were to listen to me, you might make better decisions," I said. "How is it a good idea to let some man paw you in the garden?"

Marleen's expression misted dreamily. "We made love. I don't expect a child like you to understand. We made love in the garden he's tended, among the flowers he planted."

I suppressed the urge to gag. "And the weeds he's allowed to grow. His father planted most of those flowers, anyway. Don't be a fool, Marleen."

I walked away, but as I did, she hissed after me, "You're just sorry you never let Jeff paw you in the garden, Charlie! Don't you wish you'd let my brother do more than just kiss you, you frigid bitch?"

I froze. I couldn't speak. I missed Jeff more than I'd ever missed anyone, but no, I didn't wish we'd done more. Still, her words opened up the pit of emptiness that Jeff's presence had filled before. I bowed my head.

"Shut up, Marleen." I turned to see Kyle grabbing his sister by the shoulder. "Some people have better morals than you." And he gave me an apologetic look as he led his sister away.

On Thursday, exactly a month after the trial started, the case of The State of North Carolina v. Sydney Edward Moore wound up with closing arguments by the defense and the prosecution. I wasn't present for the arguments, but I read about them on the front page of the newspaper. The prosecution charged that Sydney Moore had willfully and wrongfully murdered Tracy Collins after working at her parents' home for three weeks doing minor home repairs. The defense pled not guilty on all counts.

The more I'd read about the trial, the more I'd come to understand Sydney Moore's place in the black community. He lived with his mother, had never graduated from high school, was considered mentally handicapped. The entire black community liked him, and more than a few seemed to consider his well-being a matter of their own personal responsibility. I thought of Mrs. Broughton with Billy living just down the street. Poor Billy couldn't even have a cat because the neighborhood kids tortured it. But he'd never been accused of murder.

On Friday morning, the judge directed the jury in their obligations and sent them off to deliberate. Meanwhile, a crowd massed outside the courthouse, awaiting the verdict. This crowd grew bigger than the others, more restless, meaner. Nearby merchants locked their doors and flipped signs from "Open" to "Closed." Reporters and photographers clogged the area, patrolling the courthouse to make sure they didn't miss Sydney Moore being led back in.

At 3:32 p.m. the rumor started that the jury had reached a guilty verdict and Sydney Moore was being brought back from the jail. Excitement, anger and anticipation combined to an explosive pitch in the crowd. "He never even had a chance," a black woman cried. "He murdered a girl, what do you want?" a white woman screamed back. A white man called a black man a nigger. Somebody threw a punch. Somebody else threw a bottle. In the riot that followed, several noses, two arms, an ankle, and a third of the windows of the downtown businesses were all broken. Cars were damaged and some looting occurred. Two police officers were injured and one young girl sustained severe lacerations on her face when a bottle that was thrown landed near where she hid beneath a bench. In the newspaper, the reporter mentioned that the girl's eyes were not damaged, as if it were a blessing.

I cried when I read the newspaper report. "I told you so," Jeff said.

"Told me what?" I sniffled.

"That it would only get uglier." Jeff looked self-satisfied. "It's human nature. It's ugly."

I shook him off. Get out of my head. You left, you died. Go haunt somebody else.

"I can't," Jeff said.

"Why not?"

"Because you're the one I told everything to."

"You never told me anything," I protested. "I told you everything, but you never told me anything. Except that one thing about your grandfather."

"I told you I loved you."

"No you didn't. You said I was your girl."

"Same thing." Jeff shrugged. "And I didn't just die, I was murdered. I would never have left you."

Maybe being haunted wasn't such a bad thing. I could use supernatural help. "Who did it? Tell me who did it. Marleen says it was him, it had to be a black man."

Jeff shifted. I saw him clearly. He wanted me to know something, but he didn't want to say what. "You know better, Charlie." He faded away as Mom called me to help with the dishes.

My frequent conversations with Jeff since his death had grown more and more frustrating over time. Though he'd been far from talkative during his lifetime, death had loosened his tongue to an amazing degree. I kept these conversations secret, which was easy enough since Jeff spoke in my head and didn't need me to talk out loud.

Mom gave me a concerned look as we washed the dishes. "Are you all right?"

"Sure." I was. In fact, I was happier than I'd been since Jeff's death. In a way I had him back.

"You've been so quiet recently," Mom said. "Do you miss Jeff?"

Do I miss Jeff? It was like asking an amputee if he missed his leg. I remembered seeing Aaron Grady, a veteran of the Vietnam War, on the street one day. Aaron lost his leg in the war. The sad thing about it was he wasn't even in combat. He and some buddies were drunk, driving around in a Jeep. The Jeep overturned and Aaron was pinned underneath. They got him out and he came home, but his leg stayed in Vietnam. Nobody ever asked Aaron if he missed his leg. It would have been really dumb and pretty cruel to ask him something like that. I remembered the hollowness of his eyes mainly. Like they had nothing behind them except deep dark blackness. As if losing his leg had taken something else from him…

“Charlie.” Mom waved a soapy hand at me. “Are you still there?”

I blinked. Mom looked at me with a peculiar expression on her face. “Oh. Yeah, I mean, of course I miss Jeff, but that was like a month ago. I’m fine, Mom, really.”

“Right.” Mom nodded. “Of course. Have you seen Marleen recently?”

“Not really.” It was true. I hadn’t really seen Marleen in months.

“How come?”

I shrugged, taking a dish from the rack and rubbing the towel over it in circular motions. “I haven’t really wanted to. Marleen’s not the same anymore, Mom. She’s changed. She’s interested in things I just don’t care about.”

“I see.” After that, she was silent. In the silence, I could almost hear her internal conversation, the one she planned to have with David once I’d gone upstairs. Where she told him how much she worried about me and how I didn’t have any friends or do any of the things other kids my age were doing. She had thought I'd get over Jeff by now, but I seemed to be dwelling on him too much…

I couldn't deny she was right. Even then I knew I shouldn't be hearing Jeff's voice in my head. But that didn't change the fact that, want to or not, my dead boyfriend haunted my visions, waking and sleeping.

## Chapter Nineteen

On Monday morning, I went uptown. I knew Mom wouldn't like for me to hang around outside the courthouse after what had happened, so I took a book bag and told her I was going to the library. And I did. I spent most of the morning in the library, pretending to read while I watched out the window to see any signs of a verdict at the courthouse.

No one hung around downtown. Only press were allowed at the police barricade, which had been moved back. Double the number of uniformed officers patrolled the barricade. I noticed a number of people walking back and forth along the street. The police could keep people from loitering but they couldn't prevent them walking past.

Just before lunch, I noticed a flurry of activity at the courthouse. A police car pulled around to the back and two more parked on Main Street with their lights flashing. I saw cameras flash and men in dark suits going up the steps.

"It's time." Jeff stood at my shoulder. "If you want to see, you should go now."

So I left the library and walked up to the courthouse. Most of the way, Jeff walked beside me. By the time I got to the barricade, the police had stopped telling the milling people to move along and were concentrating on holding them back. I found a bench a block away and sat on the back so I could see better. The black-suited people had gathered at the door to the courthouse and seemed to be posing for the news cameras. I figured they were the lawyers for the defense and the district attorneys.

"They're making the most of their opportunity in the limelight," Jeff said. I pictured him perched next to me on the bench, smoking a cigarette. I could almost smell the smoke.

"Why can't you just stop smoking?" I said. "You shouldn't need to smoke anymore."

He shrugged. "Why shouldn't I smoke? I'm already dead, it can't hurt me."

"That's a really old joke."

"Yeah, but it's not everybody that can tell it." Jeff grinned at me, and I wished I could kiss him again. If I was going to haunted, why did it have to feel so lonely?

Someone in a uniform--a bailiff?--opened the door and the black-suited men and women went inside. A hush fell over the assembled crowd. Waiting was the only thing to do, so the crowd did it with all their willpower.

A light breeze ruffled my hair, drying some of the sweat that had settled on the back of my neck.

"You know, it doesn't even matter what the verdict is." Jeff blew a smoke ring at the sun.

"What do you mean?"

"It won't matter. Half the people here won't believe it, anyway. Maybe he did it. Maybe he didn't. But if you believe something strong enough, it becomes your truth, right?"

I shook my head. "The truth is the truth."

"Except when it's somebody else's truth." Jeff stuck the cigarette back into his mouth and looked at the courthouse.

A sudden wave of motion and sound went through the crowd as the courthouse door opened. Although I couldn't hear the words the bailiff uttered, it seemed like the wind wafted the word "guilty" around to all of us. The crowd gave a soft sigh and began to move away. Only one woman remained. A black woman stood by the police barricade, her skin like the bark of the oak tree out back. "Y'all know that boy didn't do it," she said. Although she didn't speak loudly, we all heard her. Her voice carried the heaviness of her conviction. She glared around at all of us, and then she turned away.

"See what I mean?" Jeff said. "When it's not your truth, you can reject it."

I rode home past the Galloway house. Kyle was outside and I stopped to speak to him. He had the hood of the Camaro up and leaned against the grille while he studied the engine.

"Hey, Charlie." He stepped back from the car, wiping his hands as I parked my bike.

"Hi." I walked over to him, uncertain why I had stopped.

Kyle motioned at the car. “Don’t have a clue what I’m doing here. She’s not running right, but I don’t know why. Jeff always took care of it.”

“Are you ready for college?” I wanted to push away any discussion of Jeff.

He flipped the stained white towel over his shoulder. “Not really. Got a lot to do, but I’ll make it.”

“Yeah,” I said.

“Tell him to take the damn car to a mechanic before he screws it up permanently.” Jeff sounded disgusted.

“You ought to take that to a mechanic.” I pointed at the Camaro.

Kyle gave me a sardonic look. “Yeah, probably. Anybody ever tell you you sound a lot like Jeff?”

“No.” I looked away. “I guess it’s to be expected, we spent so much time together.”

“Yeah.” Kyle stared off into the distance. “You’re lucky.”

“Kyle!” Mrs. Galloway stood on the top step. She waved a dishtowel at me. “Hi Charlie!”

Kyle snapped back. “Yeah Mom?”

“Have you seen your sister?” Mrs. Galloway looked around. “She said she was coming out to talk to you.”

Kyle frowned. “When? She hasn’t been out here. I haven’t seen her.”

“Oh,” Mrs. Galloway said, and something in her face shut down. “Oh, well, she probably just went for a walk, then.”

"Didn't Dad say she wasn't supposed to leave the yard?" Kyle frowned.

Mrs. Galloway brushed that away. "She's a teenage girl, Kyle, she's not going to be hemmed in by her father."

"She ought to be hemmed in by somebody," Kyle muttered, turning back to the Camaro. He slammed the hood. I felt a whoosh of warm, oily smelling air that reminded me of Jeff's skin and the inside of his metal building. Tears pricked my eyes and I looked away quickly.

"In fact," Kyle turned around and leaned on the hood of the Camaro as his mother retreated to the house, "she ought to be roped and tied. She's been going up to Whitford's every chance she gets."

I leaned on the hood next to him, my eyes drawn again to Mrs. Whitford's garden. The roses bloomed lushly and unabashedly. I remembered my dream about Jeff in Mrs. Whitford's garden. With a shock, I realized I wanted to go there desperately.

"Yes," Jeff whispered in my ear. "Go there. I can be close to you there." I felt like I'd been waiting for him to tell me, like he'd been waiting for me to remember.

I barely heard Kyle when he said he had to leave. I rode my bike to the other corner of Mrs. Whitford's garden, out of sight of the Galloway house. I walked the length of the fence, found a rock next to the fence and climbed in.

Inside, the garden was just as lush and green and full of decay as I remembered. I worked my way to the rose bushes. I closed my eyes and remembered Jeff coming to me with a rose in his hand, just as he had in my dream. I remembered the green highlights of his blue eyes, echoes of the garden's growth. The tea roses smelled wonderful if I could just filter out the smells of dead leaves. Though I knew the truth of the garden, I imagined it into something else.

"Remember what I told you about the truth," Jeff said.

I opened my eyes eagerly, but Jeff was not with me. Instead, I heard voices. Brian's. A girl's. Laughter. Was it Marleen? I raised up just enough. I didn't dare move much more. They were so close. Brian's dark hair, his small hands on the clippers. Just the other side of the rosebushes. And the other hair, smooth and blond. Not Marleen's riot of curls. Brian clipped a rose from the bush and held it out. She turned a little, a smile playing on her curved lips. Not Marleen. Dominique Grady.

"That's the truth," Jeff said.

I wasn't sure what to do with the truth Jeff had given me. I debated it all the way home. Where was Marleen while Brian was with Dominique? Had Brian even let Marleen back inside his house since she'd been back? It didn't seem likely. And Dominique. This explained why she'd asked me whether Marleen was coming back. Marleen had no interest in cheerleading, but

Dominique was interested in Brian. I shivered at the thought of what Brian was doing to another young girl.

After dinner, I went to bed. I didn't want to think about Marleen or Brian anymore. I heard Mom and David's voices downstairs. Mom sounded upset and David soothing. The rise and fall of their voices was like the ocean surf washing in to cover me, then retreating. Eventually, the surf came in and covered me completely in darkness.

I swam to the surface and emerged in Mrs. Whitford's garden. Brian Whitford stood at the other end of the garden, but his back was to me and he stood as still as a statue. Vines twined around his blue jean-clad legs, as if they were taking him over, drawing him into the garden and making him a part of its darkness.

"There's more secrets here." Jeff stood beside me. "There's more truth. You have to look closer."

I looked closer at Brian's hands. Beneath each small rounded nail was a crescent of crimson. I stepped back. Just paint, it's only paint. But red dripped from the nails. It ran in rivulets down his legs and the vines drank it, sucked it up and reached for more…

I woke screaming.

Mom took me back to see Mrs. Godfrey.

"You've had some pretty tragic things happen to you in the past few months," Mrs. Godfrey said.

I frowned. I didn't want to be there and I didn't care if she knew. "They didn't happen to me."

"To people you know and love, then." Mrs. Godfrey wasn't about to be sidetracked. "Sometimes that's even worse."

"You don't know the half of it." I pulled my legs up into my chair, suddenly feeling the shadows creeping up all my exposed skin.

"Tell me. I want to know."

"Where should I start?" I hesitated, despairing of ever finding a good place to begin, but then I started and as I talked, I pieced it all together. I told her about Marleen's obsession with an older man, about Tracy's murder and Kyle being a suspect. I told her about how I watched Marleen's family and home fall apart, even as I found a friend and someone to talk to in Jeff. I told her how it made me feel when Jeff called me his girl, how safe I felt belonging with someone. How we became suspicious of Brian Whitford and tipped the police off. How that led to Mrs. Collins confronting Brian and her subsequent breakdown. Sydney Moore's arrest, Kyle's exoneration, Jeff's murder. Everything that had happened over the past year was a piece of a crazy quilt that hadn't been sewn together yet. Some pieces fit with others, but some didn't.

Mrs. Godfrey listened, nodding her head. "And where do you fit in?" she asked as if she could read my mind.

"I told you." I shook my head, not sure what she was asking me.

"So the only things going on in your life involve these other people?" Mrs. Godfrey raised her eyebrows. "You don't have any unresolved issues of your own?"

I thought of the slip of paper in my music box. Every crisis had brought me back to that tiny piece of information about myself. An unresolved issue. But the resolution of that issue could affect everyone from me and Mom to David and Dougie.

"There is something," Mrs. Godfrey said into the silence.

"Yeah." I nodded, reluctant to admit it. "There's one thing. But I think I know what to do about it."

I went home. I found some magazines and tore some pages out. Newspaper would work, too, but I knew magazines were better. Upstairs, I grabbed my music box and took out the envelope. Then I tore it open, closed my eyes and groped inside for the sliver of paper. Without looking, I hurried downstairs and out to the pond. The boat I'd made from the magazine pages would float for a while. I'd made them before. Sometimes they floated all the way to the middle of the pond before they sank. Sometimes they even floated back to the bank.

I folded the sliver of paper securely into the pages. I pictured a little man waving to me from the deck of a tiny boat.

Nameless and faceless. “If he comes back to you, he’s yours, then?” Jeff said.

I didn’t answer. I launched the boat and watched as the wind caught it and pushed it toward the middle of the pond. I wondered where it would go. Would it come back? “Do you want it to come back?” Jeff asked.

A turtle raised its head from the water beside the boat. Tiny ripples made the vessel dip and sway in the murky water. The tiny man on the boat deck waved his arms in alarm. I thought of what might happen if my father came back into my life, how my mother would react, how David would feel.

The turtle, curious, moved closer, looking more like a sea monster than ever next to the tiny boat. Again the little man appealed to me for help. I could wade out and save him. But without a face to focus on, I found it difficult to find enough sympathy for him to warrant getting my feet wet. The ripples got bigger and then a gust of wind brushed past, pushing the boat too far to its starboard. It toppled and began taking on water.

I watched as the little man went underwater--still not too late--came up--soaked through now--and went under again and again. He bobbed there a moment, then relinquished whatever hope for life he still held and went under a final time.

“Good.” Jeff stood and brushed his jeans off, then walked away.

I stayed a little longer, enjoying the quiet summer afternoon.

## Chapter Twenty

I wanted to tell Mom she didn't have to worry about me contacting my father any more, but I couldn't find the words. Of course, she could still have given me the name and address again, but with my symbolic drowning of my father, I had put that option away forever.

After dinner, I plunged my hands into the dishwater and brought up a soapy dish. I ran the dishcloth over the soiled surface, wiping away the remains of dinner. Then I rinsed the soapy residue away and handed the plate to Mom to dry. I felt more energetic than I had since Jeff died and when one of my favorite songs came on the radio, I started singing along.

"You're chipper." Mom smiled and put an arm around my shoulders.

"Yeah, I guess." I paused a moment, thinking. "Mom, do you remember that park you used to take me to? The one with a really high slide that went around and around in circles."

"Sure." She put the dish away. "I remember you wouldn't go down the slide by yourself. You always wanted me to go with you."

"I think Dougie would like it there," I said. "I could go down the slide with him, if he was scared. Maybe we could have a picnic there."

Mom smiled. "Yes, that would be nice. David would like it, too, I imagine."

"Sure." I handed her another plate. "Let's talk to Dad about it later."

Mom froze at my use of the word "Dad", but then she carefully dried the plate and put it on the shelf. "Let's do that."

That night I dreamed about Mrs. Whitford's garden again. The dream was different, but at the same time, it was the same. Snakes rather than vines crawled up Brian Whitford's frozen legs. And Jeff showed up more clearly than before. As if he'd moved closer to me … or I to him. When I woke, sweating but not screaming, I wrote down every aspect of the dream in my dream journal. Everything I could remember. I wasn't sure if it was Jeff or my own psyche that was trying to tell me something, and in fact, I was no longer certain how to tell the two apart.

I did the same thing night after night. In the mornings, I would read what I'd written, but it still made no sense. Maybe I had just lost my senses and the nightmare meant nothing in particular.

"You know better than that." Jeff sat on my bed beside me. "Cute PJ's."

"Shut up." Grumpy from lack of sleep, I wasn't even happy to see him. "If you're so smart, tell me what the dream means."

He looked at me solemnly, no trace of teasing. “It means you can’t trust anybody. You know what it means. I’ve already told you.”

“Tell me again.”

“It is the key to salvation and damnation.”

I rolled my eyes. “I liked you better when you smoked more than you talked.”

He didn’t reply, but I remembered again what it had felt like to kiss him, and I wished he was really there.

The next Monday morning, I rode my bike over to the Galloway house. Kyle’s Camaro was gone and so was his dad’s truck. Mrs. Galloway and Marleen were alone in the house. I parked my bike on the other side of Mrs. Whitford’s garden, snuck in and waited.

A blue jay landed on a tree nearby. He cocked his head from one side to the other. I remembered hearing that a blue jay’s feathers are not really blue but simply refract light in a way that makes them appear so in the sunlight. I looked at the jay with his brilliant markings and found it difficult to believe. He screamed and took off, calling a warning to any unwary animals nearby. Human here, he called. Beware!

Movement at the edge of the garden attracted my eyes. I sat up, careful to stay just below the rhododendron bushes and peering past their broad, flat leaves. Pink and white blossoms had just begun to burst through their buds.

Marleen slipped through the gate, glanced back at her house and then worked her way through the garden, not bothering to conceal herself. No doubt she hoped Brian would see her. She wore cutoff denim shorts with strings hanging down her thighs and a white blouse unbuttoned a little too far. Her curly blond hair was loose down her back and fell well past her shoulder blades. I wondered if she was trying to grow it long enough to sit on. She'd always said she wanted hair long enough to sit on. Her room was papered with pictures of Crystal Gayle torn from magazines. I want hair that long, she'd say. It's so romantic. Marleen sat on a gray stone, holding her head like a queen.

Jeff peered past me. "She wants Brian to see her."

"No kidding."

The back door of the Whitford house opened. Brian Whitford came out. He paused and picked up a hoe. I watched as he worked his way through the garden to where Marleen sat, his small hand clutching the hoe. I tensed. Would he hurt Marleen? I knew he didn't want her there. He had Dominique now. I started to push my way through the undergrowth.

"Where are you going?" Jeff's voice sounded alarmed.

"Closer to your sister." I glared at him. "She might need help."

"What would you do?" Jeff asked and I stopped.

Marleen stood as Brian came toward her holding the hoe over his shoulder. She started toward him, but he held his hand out, palm facing her. She stopped and I saw her face, her eyes pleading. He shook his head. I could hear their voices, but just barely. He sounded stern. He pointed at her house. Go on, scram. She shook her head, and I could tell she was crying now. She reached for him, but he pulled away, pushed her back. She fell, and now I could hear her crying. I winced. I understood that she was hurting, but I knew I could never understand what she was doing. She'd gone somewhere in her heart and mind where I would never be able to follow her.

"Mom should never have brought her home." Jeff stood at my shoulder, watching.

I agreed. I watched as Brian walked away and Marleen sat crying on the ground. I wanted to go to her, but I knew she'd never forgive me. Spying. Brian went back inside. Marleen stayed where she was for several minutes, sitting on the ground, her head hanging, her legs splayed out in front of her. She looked like a small child. I could no longer hear her sobs, but her shoulders jerked every now and then, a spasmodic movement. The screen door of the Galloway house slammed and Marleen jerked at the sound. She glanced over at her house, at something I could not see, then stood and slipped through the bushes back to the garden gate. I watched her walk the long way around her house, trying to look like she was coming from another direction if her mother caught her.

"It's really over, then." I drew in a deep breath, ready to expel it in a relieved sigh.

"Not quite." His voice was soft, a tickle on my eardrum.

I remembered the dream and looked at the top of the garden. Brian was inside. Was he watching? Could I do what I needed to do without him seeing me? I slipped through the rhododendrons with their broad, flat, sticky leaves that clung to my skin to the rose bushes with the thorns that scratched at me to a wide flat expanse of flowerbed. At the top of this bed Brian had stood in my dream. I could even see the vines spreading out like long fingers along the border.

The exact spot Brian had stood in my dream was too exposed and easy to see from the Whitford house, but I worked my way around so I crouched behind the bushes directly behind the spot. "Right there," Jeff whispered, and I stopped.

I could see more of the Whitford house, including the back steps. But in my dream, Brian had been looking slightly to the left, away from the house. I looked left, tracing his line of vision as nearly as possible. I could see two old stumps, as dark from age as if they'd been varnished, from some trees Mr. Whitford had taken out. Beyond them, a birdbath, neglected since Mrs, Whitford's death. Beyond that, a dilapidated old garage, falling apart in spaces, the wood gray and peeling. "I don't understand." I looked at Jeff. "What am I supposed to see?"

"Sometimes it's not what you see but what you suspect," he said. "What do you suspect Brian is capable of doing?"

I didn't hesitate. "Murder. You know that. But they've arrested Tracy's murderer. Brian didn't do it."

"Is Tracy the only murder victim you know?" Jeff raised his eyebrows.

The implication made me sit down on the dark earth of the flowerbed, the air sucked from me so suddenly I felt my stomach collapse in on itself. "You mean you? Did Brian murder you?"

Jeff didn't answer. I was alone. Not even a ghost to keep me company. I searched for a path to the garage. I had to get in there. If I used the woods that bordered the garden for cover, I might be able to make it without being spotted. I slipped back to the edge, over the fence and into the woods. I approached the garage on the side away from the house.

It was an old-fashioned garage, more of a wooden carport with sides, really. No door. Brian's bike was parked next to a conglomeration of junk. I'd seen him riding it often enough in town. To the best of my knowledge, he didn't own a car. But he'd have needed something bigger than a bike to run Jeff and his Vespa off the road. Beyond the bike, a collection of hubcaps, holes rusting through the once shiny metal, were the only real sign of a car. Several gas cans, a bottle of antifreeze, what looked like a pitchfork and three yard rakes. A rusty old shovel lay on its side. Two bike frames missing their wheels leaned against the left side of the garage and a lawnmower and chainsaw were on the right side. I worked my way past them all, my hands in front of me to ward off cobwebs. Halfway to the back, I paused beside a molding formica dining table as it occurred to me I hadn't encountered a single web. I lowered my arms, my heart beating faster, and I pushed through the decaying objects until I found myself at the back of the garage, facing a large object covered by a faded blue tarp.

Not large enough for a car, but… I drew back the tarp with a flourish that sent dust motes dancing in the sunlight that came through a hole in the age-frosted windowpane, the only window in the garage. I coughed and backed away. The dust cloud swirled in my vision, blinding me, but I saw it anyway.

A motorcycle. An old one, but well preserved. I didn't know much about motorcycles, but I figured Jeff would've liked this one. Silver and black, it gleamed in the semi-darkness of the garage. A diamond in a coalmine, the motorcycle was the one thing without a sign of decay. I wondered if it was Brian's … or had it been Mr. Whitford's secret passion? When he wasn't out in his garden, was he back here polishing the motorcycle? Somehow I found it easier to imagine Brian in that role, but then, I'd never known Mr. Whitford all that well. He appreciated pretty flowers and beautiful women, why not machines?

This machine was near perfect, too. I ran my finger over the shining polished chrome. Only a slight scratch here and there until my finger snagged on something on the tailpipe. Leaning down, I examined the deep gouges, which could only have been caused by the tailpipe meeting the pavement.

In a flash, I saw what might have happened. Brian happening upon Jeff while riding his motorcycle, or even waiting for Jeff to pass. Swooping down on the much slower, less graceful Vespa, pushing him over to the side of the road. Jeff would have fought back, maybe Brian didn't even intend to kill him. The Vespa and the motorcycle clashing, tangling, Jeff pulling Brian down with him. But Brian broke loose at the last moment, avoided the crash. I saw Jeff's head hit the pavement and remembered he hadn't worn a helmet. I saw a trail of blood running through the rough pavement, and before it touched his shoe, Brian got both wheels underneath him again and left the scene.

"I've been meaning to fix that."

I jumped and whirled. Brian leaned casually in the doorway. "The scratch," he said, motioning toward the tailpipe. "It's a shame to mar such a beautiful thing with an ugly jagged mark like that."

I swallowed hard. Dancing golden motes of dust filled the air, but the two of us remained still and perfectly quiet. It felt like what I'd always imagined being stuck in the middle of a city street during rush hour might feel like. I couldn't see a way out, either. If he had murdered Tracy and Jeff, he wouldn't hesitate to murder me, too. But I couldn't think of a way to get out of the garage, or even a way to explain my presence.

"Where is Marleen?" I blurted the best thing I could think of.

Brian stepped toward me, and I backed away. I could see his smile as he grasped the tarp, drawing it over the motorcycle. "She's not hiding under a tarp in my garage," he said. "I only keep my dad's old motorcycle here."

"She was here earlier." I lifted my chin, determined to show no fear.

Brian sighed and shook his head. "She was in the garden again. Trespassing. I sent her home. That child has gotten me into enough trouble as it is." He paused, looking down at the Galloway house. "Parental supervision would do her a world of good. I know it did me."

He grinned at me, but there was nothing friendly in the grin. Brittle, ice-edged, like a pond that's frozen over but waiting to break. He took a step away from the door, a step toward me. "You know what my father used to do to me to punish me?" Without waiting for an answer, he went on, and I imagined the cracks spreading across the brittle ice of his face. "He had this belt with spikes in it, from back when he rode his motorcycle. If he believed I needed to be punished, he'd put that belt around my neck and tighten it up so those spikes poked into my neck every time I breathed. It didn't hurt at first, but after a couple of hours, it got to be downright irritating." His eyes reflected the light of the sun. I couldn't see into them. He took another step toward me, lowering his voice. "I still have that belt, you know. Would you like to see it, Charlie?"

"Run, Charlie," Jeff whispered in my ear. I didn't need the advice. I couldn't stay there any longer. In spite of the close quarters and my reluctance to go anywhere near him, I raced past Brian into the open afternoon. I thought I heard him laughing behind me, but I didn't stop running until I was well down the block, away from him, away from the motorcycle I now suspected had killed Jeff, away from the darkness in the garage and house and under the flowers in the garden.

## Chapter Twenty-One

I tried my damnedest to forget the motorcycle and the scene with Brian, but it haunted me worse than Jeff had, when he'd been there. He'd gone now. Maybe he'd done what he needed to do. Sometimes I was relieved, sometimes I wished him well and every now and then, I cursed him for leaving me with the knowledge he'd given me.

What was I supposed to do with it? I was 13 years old, barely grown out of my childhood. Who was going to listen to me? And I had no doubt that Brian was already erasing the evidence from the motorcycle. A little sanding and polishing and the scratch would be gone. He wouldn't need any help, he wouldn't need any replacement parts. Nothing that would leave a trail.

Did the police know it was a motorcycle that had driven Jeff off the road? I hadn't read anything about it in the newspaper, but I'd heard about the police not telling the newspapers everything about the evidence they'd found. So that if somebody confessed to the crime, it could be confirmed by what they knew about it.

Brian Whitford wasn't going to confess.

In my dreams now, Brian Whitford stood in his garden, frozen like before, but now it was metal studded belts that held him in place. And his fingers no longer sprouted fountains of blood, but when I looked at his face, a tear of blood ran down his frozen cheek. At least, that's what happened in my sleeping dreams.

In my waking hours, I'd find myself on the Vespa with Jeff. My cheek was pressed against his shoulder. I could smell motor oil and fresh cut grass. From the darkness behind us I heard a roar of a powerful engine. Glancing over my shoulder, all I could see was an enormous bright light coming closer and closer. Drawing alongside, tangling, smashing metal, a moment of flight, a moment of terror, then blackness.

Mom sensed something wrong with me when I started giving a start of terror at odd times like meals or during conversations or at night when we'd all be sitting on the couch together watching Dougie play on the floor. She wanted me to go back to see Mrs. Godfrey, but ever since I'd drowned my father's name, I'd known I could solve my own problems. Even this one. I had the knowledge but I had to decide what to do with it.

For three straight days, I rode my bicycle to Mrs. Whitford's garden and hid among the weeds and bushes by the road while I watched for Marleen. Every day I saw her either sneaking in or out of the garden. I had no illusions about her meeting Brian anymore, although I was sure that's what she'd tell me she was doing.

On the fourth day, I saw her going in and I followed her. It was Independence Day, the fourth of July. That night, there would be fireworks downtown. Everyone would go. The town's three big firetrucks would be brought out for admiration. They'd be primed and ready for excitement. Mom and David were planning to go. They'd lather Dougie in mosquito repellent and take him.

I planned to tell them I was meeting a friend. Marleen.

I didn't plan to lie.

I worked my way to a little hill where I could see Marleen. I'd decided I didn't care if Brian saw me. I didn't care if Marleen saw me either. It was time to set Marleen free of the hold Brian had over her.

Marleen didn't see me. I watched as she snuck through the rose bushes and hedges to a large pine tree near the house. I remembered the pine needles I'd seen tangled in her hair. Sure enough, Marleen slid under the lowest hanging branch.

I followed her. I didn't bother with concealment. Brian could have hurt me before when he saw me in the garage, when he knew what I knew. He hadn't, and he hadn't come after me since. I'd decided what he'd done to Jeff had been an accident. If the embankment at that particular spot of road hadn't been so steep, if Jeff had been wearing a helmet, if the clash of the motorcycle with the Vespa hadn't been so violent, Jeff would have been hurt and maybe scared (more likely angry) but not killed. Not dead.

So Brian probably wasn't a murderer. Maybe he wasn't psychopathic.

Regardless, he needed to be punished, and I needed Marleen to help me take care of that.

"Hi." I slid under the pine tree branches next to Marleen.

"Shit!" She gasped. Then she laughed, a little hysterical edge to her laughter. "You scared me."

"I'll bet." I nodded toward the house. "Is Dominique in there?"

"Who?" Marleen pretended not to know what I was talking about.

"Dominique." I tried to speak in a no-nonsense tone like my mom did with me. "You know, tall, leggy blond. Cheerleader type. I saw her go in there a couple of times. I figure that's why she was so concerned about you when you went to Chicago."

"She was?" Marleen blinked.

"Yeah." I cupped my chin in my hand. "She said you were thinking of becoming a cheerleader. She said you guys had talked about it."

"We didn't!" Marleen said. "I've never wanted to be a cheerleader. You know that."

"Do I?" I shrugged. "I don't know that I know that much about you, anymore. Seriously. I mean, we've barely spoken since you got back and you're always up here."

Marleen looked away. "I know. And I was really mean after Jeff died, Charlie. I'm sorry. Kyle told me about how much Jeff changed when you guys started hanging out together. Kyle says Jeff really cared a lot about you."

I felt a knot tighten in my chest, but I swallowed it. I hadn't cried since Jeff's funeral. I didn't plan to start again now. "Yeah. So are you over this Brian Whitford thing, then?" As if we weren't hiding under a  pine tree in his yard.

"Absolutely." As if she hadn't been coming here all summer.

"Good." I gave her a narrow look. "Because I think he killed Jeff."

Marleen shook her head. "Impossible. The police said it was some black trying to get back at Kyle for pinning Tracy's murder on one of them."

"Kyle didn't pin Tracy's murder on anybody." I knew she was making it up. She didn't know any more about what the police thought than I did.

"Of course not." She looked confused. "I mean, I know that. But that's what they think. They think white people are out to get them or something."

I wasn't totally certain "they" were wrong, but I also wasn't ready to take up this conversation with Marleen. I guided the conversation back to where I needed it to be. "It wasn't a black. It was Brian. I found a motorcycle in his garage. It was scratched."

"Scratched?" Marleen laughed. "How old was it? I bet it was old Mr. Whitford's. He probably was the last one to ride it, so I bet it's got some scratches on it."

"No." It felt surreal lying on my belly on a scratchy bed of pine needles with a low bough of pine branches just above my head telling my former best friend that her former boyfriend had killed her brother. I drew in a deep breath of piney smelling air and continued. "It was perfect, seriously. Like somebody had worked on it really recently. Painted and polished and everything. Except that one scratch. It felt like road rash."

"So Brian took it out joyriding and wrecked it. He's lucky he didn't kill himself." She shrugged, trying to sound like she didn't care.

"No." How could I make her understand? "You know after you left, Brian was really upset about it. Did you tell him it was me and Jeff who called the police?"

Marleen looked away again. "Yeah, I guess. I'm sorry."

"It's okay. But Brian cornered me and made all kinds of threats and then Mrs. Collins attacked him. I figure maybe he wanted to scare me. And maybe he wanted to scare Jeff, too."

Marleen gulped. I could see she was starting to believe me. She moved a little closer. "Have you called the police?"

I shook my head. "They'd never believe me. Plus, there's no real evidence. There's the scratch, but I think Brian's probably already taken care of that. If I call the police, they'll just think I don't like him because of what he did to you."

Marleen looked at me sharply, but stayed quiet.

I decided the truth would help me here. "And they'd be right."

"Oh Charlie." Marleen looked relieved. "Really?"

"Really." I still hadn't lied. I did hate Brian for what he'd done to Marleen, and I disliked her nearly as much for allowing it. But I could get over that if she'd help me with what needed to be done.

She reached out for me and hugged me. "I've missed you so much. There's nobody in Chicago like you. There's nobody like you here, either, for that matter." I hugged her back, perhaps not as fiercely, but maybe she excused that because we were nearly covered in pine needles as it was.

Marleen sniffled as she drew away, wiping her eyes with the back of her hand. "So what are you going to do?"

"I'm going to show him I'm not scared of him." I explained my plan for punishing Brian. As I spoke, her eyes glimmered. I could sense a certain satisfaction in her. She wanted to punish Brian, too, maybe for what he'd done to Jeff, but mostly for what he'd done to her. I realized I still didn't know that whole story and probably never would. It didn't matter.

"I can do it on my own," I said when I'd finished. "I don't really need help, but I thought since Jeff was your brother, it would only be fair to offer you the chance."

"I'll help." Her voice was firm. "Tell me what I need to do."

"Meet me back here at eight thirty. I want to make sure Brian leaves to go to the fireworks. It's important that he not be here." I paused. "Oh, and tell your mom we're going to meet at the fireworks. That's what I'm telling my mom. She'll be thrilled. She's been wanting me to patch things up with you for a while."

"Yeah, mine too." She paused, her eyes on the Whitford house. "I'll take care of it."

As she rolled out from under the pine tree and headed back down to her house, I realized Independence Day was about to take on a whole new meaning for Marleen Galloway.

Mom was just as thrilled as I'd known she would be. In fact, she was still talking about how wonderful it was when she put Dougie's shoes on his feet as she and David were getting ready to leave. "Of course, I understand where you were coming from, Charlie. Marleen definitely had problems, and she let them get the better of her friendship with you. But she's over them now, and you can move on. Girls need best friends. You're lucky to have Marleen."

"Yeah, I know, Mom," I said. David walked by behind her and rolled his eyes at me. I grinned.

Mom looked over her shoulder. "You cut it out. I don't need you undermining my authority like that." She hit him with a burp towel. Things had improved between Mom and David recently. I liked that.

"You be careful." Mom kissed me on the nose as they left.

"I will." I waved and shut the door. Still half an hour before I had to meet Marleen. I paced. With every step, I felt a charge of resolve shoot up my leg to my faltering heart, strengthening me. I wanted to dismiss Brian, but to do that, I had to make sure he wouldn't ever be a problem for me again. Like castration for a rapist, the punishment I had in mind should suit Brian.

When time came to leave, I left.

Marleen wasn't immediately visible when I approached Mrs. Whitford's garden. Did she chicken out? Had she called the cops?

"Pssst, Charlie!" Marleen waved to me from the woods bordering the garden. Relief surged over me. I was glad I wouldn't have to do this alone. "He's still there. Are you sure he'll go to the fireworks?"

"Yeah." I hunkered down beside her. "Everybody goes to the fireworks, so he's bound to go, too. It's sort of his way of keeping up appearances."

Together we watched the front of the house. I was absolutely certain I was right and Brian would go to the fireworks. I knew he did his best to appear normal in every way he could. Perhaps it was something he'd learned long ago, if his father had truly been as cruel as he said. He probably imagined everyone in town was against him, that we suspected he was a deviant personality, and so he tried twice as hard to fit in. That was why he'd gone to the sidewalk sale. Because everyone went to sidewalk sales.

Five minutes later, Brian emerged from his house. Sticking his hands in his pockets, he sauntered up the road.

"Wait." I stopped Marleen when she started to rise. "Make sure he's gone."

Marleen was silent and still for a moment. "How is this going to work, again?"

"He's a bully," I said. "Maybe because his dad was a bully, but that's no excuse. He tried to bully me, and he tried to bully Jeff. He went too far and Jeff died. Now it's time for me to show him he can't act this way with us. If we show him we're not scared, if we do something spectacular that's meant to scare him, he'll back off."

"But it won't get him arrested." Marleen looked troubled. "He won't have to pay for murdering Jeff."

"I told you." I fought for patience. "He didn't murder Jeff. It was an accident. Brian was just trying to scare Jeff."

"You don't know that for sure." Marleen's voice got a little louder.

I sighed. "Whatever, Marleen. But look, tonight we're just here to scare him. Tomorrow you can call the police or whatever you want. Just concentrate on what we're doing tonight."

"Right." She nodded, seeming refocused.

I thought I knew what was going on with Marleen. She didn't want revenge for Jeff. She wanted revenge for herself. Which was okay, and I could use that, but I needed her to remember my plan.

Brian hadn't returned, so I decided it was okay to get started. We snuck out of the woods and crept toward the garage. Just as we were nearly there, I heard voices, grabbed Marleen and ducked inside the garage door. We stood frozen, pressed against the side of the garage, hiding from the last of the summer evening light as a group of people from the neighborhood trooped past.

When they were gone, I breathed a sigh of relief. It was nearly dark. I could see fireflies lighting up under the darkest bushes and trees. The streetlight on the corner came on, providing me with just enough light to pick my way back to the corner where I'd seen the gas cans. As I'd hoped, they were full. I uncapped one and sniffed, then coughed as the gasoline fumes slid down my airways. "Okay, let's get this done." I turned but Marleen was not at my side. "Marleen?"

"Here." She stood beside the motorcycle, pulling at the tarp. "I want to see it." She knelt beside the motorcycle. It looked surprisingly small beside her. In my memory I'd blown it up to amazing proportions, but in reality, I realized it was just a small thing. A car could blow past it and knock it over without effort, a semi-trailer could flatten it. In fact, I imagined I could reach out with one finger and knock it off its kickstand. Marleen ran her fingers lovingly over the handlebars, the gas tank, the seat, down to the tailpipe. I saw her shoulders jerk as her fingers encountered the scratched tailpipe. She looked over her shoulder at me. "It's still there."

"It doesn't matter." I motioned impatiently. "Come on! We've got to get started."

As if to emphasize my words, the first fireworks exploded in a shower of red and green sparks. I held out a gas can to Marleen, and she came over to me and took it. "Okay." She still sounded reluctant.

I had only a very vague idea of how to start a fire, but I figured if you had enough gas (and we conveniently did) and dry timber (the garage was made of it), you couldn't really go wrong. I directed Marleen to splash gas on one wall while I did the other. "Don't get any on you." I tossed a wooden crate against the wall and doused it. "And throw anything wood against the wall. It'll help it burn." Marleen just nodded.

When I finished, the fumes were nearly overpowering. I hadn't thought to bring anything to put over my nose and mouth. I staggered back outside to the fresh air. "Marleen!" I called, fearing she'd been overcome by the fumes. I took a long deep breath of air as I prepared to launch myself back into the garage. But just then she also staggered out and collapsed on the grass a few feet away. I relaxed. "Good."

I turned back, pulling the pack of matches out of my pocket. Lighting one, I tossed it in and watched blue curls of flame begin to work their way up the wall. I glanced at Marleen as I lit another match. She raised herself to a sitting position, a pensive look on her face. I wondered if she felt guilty. I didn't. I didn't feel the victorious glory I'd imagined, either. I felt numb and relieved that it was nearly over. I turned to throw the other match and felt a whoosh of air behind me just as the match left my hand. "What?" I turned back. Marleen no longer sat on the grass. I looked around, swiveling back and forth. What happened to her? Where did she go? "Marleen!" In my excitement, I forgot I'd just set fire to the garage. Wood splintered and crackled and suddenly I knew where Marleen was.

"Marleen!" I yelled into the garage. The matches fell from my paralyzed fingers and flames curled, reaching into the depths of blackness where my friend had just disappeared. "Marleen! No!"

Someone ran up behind me. "What is it? How did this happen?" A man. He grabbed me around the waist as I tried to hurl myself into the garage.

"She's in there," I screamed, fighting his grip. "She went in there!"

"Dear God." The man released me and pulled his shirt off to beat at the flames. Even as he did it, a shadow emerged from the flames, bigger than Marleen. Too big. A shadow monster, something too evil, something released from the aged wood by the heat of the fire. I fell to the ground. I could hear the sirens of the fire engine and more explosions above my head, smell the burning wood, and feel the hard gravel under my knees. I could make sense of all those things, but what I saw made no sense at all.

Then I saw the man running forward, grabbing the monster and tearing it to pieces. He pulled a third of the monster away and the other part fell over onto the gravel drive. I stared in dumbfounded amazement at the motorcycle fallen over on its side and Marleen doubled over, coughing and choking on the smoke. The man brought her over to sit next to where I'd fallen. He yelled at somebody to bring water as red and blue lights began to wash over us.

"I want to know what happened here," the policeman said somewhere between a few seconds and an hour later. Two firemen poked around the smoking remains of the garage. Several others gathered beside the fire truck, talking in low voices. A crowd had assembled, more excited by this tiny fire than they'd been by the fireworks display. Three other policemen held them back at the end of the drive.

I wasn't sure how to answer. In all the different scenarios I'd imagined, getting caught had never figured in. What would Mom and David say? Was setting fire to a neighbor's garage a misdemeanor or a felony? Would I go to jail? I saw Brian Whitford speaking to one of the policemen. I had to say something, so I opened my mouth, but Marleen beat me to it.

“He killed my brother.” Her voice was low and hoarse from the coughing.

“What?” The policeman didn’t seem able to process the information.

“My brother.” Marleen drew the word “brother” out, as if she were speaking to someone mentally slow. “Jeff Galloway. You remember him? Y’all tried to convince us we’d never find out who killed him, who ran him off the road. But Charlie figured it out. She found the motorcycle. It’s got a scratch on the tailpipe.”

“Oh God.” I covered my face with my hands. Marleen had obviously lost it.

“Check it out,” the policeman said to his partner, who went over and ran his hand along the tailpipe. He glanced back and nodded. “So,” the officer said. “It has a scratch. A lot of motorcycles probably have scratches on them.”

“Brian did it.” Her voice rose. “He told me he’d kill anyone who tried to keep us apart.” I looked at her. Marleen hadn’t mentioned that. “So when he found out Jeff was the one who called you guys anonymously and told you to search his house, he was angry. I think he just meant to scare Jeff, but he ended up killing him. He killed my brother and I want you to arrest him!” Her voice rose, but because she was hoarse, it ended on a screech and faded into another bout of coughing.

“How did the garage catch fire?” The policeman looked at us suspiciously.

I opened my mouth to answer again, but Marleen dug her nails into my arm, still coughing too hard to reply. "I-I--"

"I did it," Marleen gasped through her coughs. She took another sip of water and slowly the coughing subsided as the policemen waited impatiently.

"You set fire to the garage and then went back inside to get the motorcycle?" I could understand the officer's doubts. I still couldn't believe Marleen had gone back inside the burning tinderbox of the garage. I remembered my horror when I'd turned and seen she was gone. I shivered, cold in spite of the eighty-degree summer heat.

"I changed my mind." Marleen shrugged. Her voice was low, and she looked down. "I set fire to the garage for revenge. But then I realized I was destroying the only evidence that could link the son-of-a-bitch to my brother's death, so I ran back inside to get the motorcycle."

The policemen looked at each other. "Go call it in," said the first one. "Detective Padgett's working that case. He'll want to come down here." He turned back to me as his partner walked back to the patrol car. "And where do you come into this story?"

Again Marleen beat me to it. "She came to try to stop me. She knew what I was going to do and she came just in time to see me run back into the garage. She wanted me to call the police in the first place, but I thought I could handle it on my own." She broke off, her fingers still digging into my arm. I looked desperately for my voice, but I couldn't find it before Marleen spoke again, and this time real tears rolled down her face as she looked at me. "Charlie's never been anything but a good friend to me. She tried to tell me Brian was trouble. She tried to warn me. But I wouldn't listen. I never have. I've been an awful friend to her, but I'm going to be better."

She broke off and pulled me into a hug. "Go with it," she whispered in my ear.

"Is that true?" the policeman asked.

"Uh, yeah." Marleen released me. I thought I saw her wink. This gift from my friend was unexpected, but I grasped at it and held on by my fingernails. "Pretty much."

The policeman turned and motioned to another officer, who brought Brian Whitford over. "About time," Brian said. "What the hell's going on here? I go out for an hour and come back to find half my property destroyed. What kind of neighborhood is this?" His eyes swept over us, leaving me feeling even colder.

"The kind of neighborhood where you get arrested for murder, you bastard," Marleen hissed.

He glared at her, but the policeman pointed at the bike, drawing his attention away. "That your bike, Mr. Whitford?

Brian looked at the motorcycle. "Yes, I mean, it was my father's. I don't ride it, but it was one of his prized possessions. Probably the only thing of value in that garage. I'm glad to see somebody saved it." His voice sounded calm, but I saw his eyes flickering around, as if he were searching for a way out.

"We're going to have to impound it," the policeman said. "If you'll just bring me your registration, I'll give you a receipt."

"Impound it?" Brian glared at the officer, looking like a trapped animal. "Why?"

"We have information that the bike may have been used in a crime," the policeman said.

"I told you, I don't ride it." Brian shifted from one foot to another.

"Regardless," the policeman said. "If you'll just get me that registration, Mr. Whitford."

Brian faced him. "You can't take anything without a warrant."

"I can take care of that," the policeman said. "I thought you might want to cooperate. You see, during a recent hit-and-run, a motorcycle left one hell of a skid mark. If we can just take your bike down to the precinct and compare it to the photos and impressions we took, we could probably clear it immediately."

Brian looked at the policeman and the policeman looked at Brian. I remembered once when I saw a cat that had fallen down a hole somebody had dug for a fencepost they'd never put in. The cat's hindquarters were stuck down the hole, its head and front paws outside, scrabbling furiously at the ground. It hadn't been able to help itself and anybody who came near enough to try to help it had been scratched and bitten. Finally, animal control had come and a man with long leather gloves had plucked the cat out of the hole by the scruff of the neck and tossed it into a cage in the back of his truck. Brian had that same defiant, terrified looked in his eyes.

"Fine," Brian said after several seconds. "I'll get the registration."

The policeman turned back to us. "I'll call your parents. Miss Galloway, you'll have to come down to the station after we have you checked out at the emergency room." He looked at me. "We'll take you home, but the detective may have some questions for you later on." He nodded to Marleen, who started to get up. I realized I was still holding her hand. I gave it one final squeeze as she stood, and then I let go.

I watched as an officer led Marleen to the police car. I realized I hadn't told her about drowning my father's name, and I wished I'd confessed to her how much Jeff had meant to me. Just as Marleen slid into the backseat of the car, I opened my mouth but I couldn't think of a way to tell her everything in the last second before the car door closed, so I shut my mouth again.

Brian Whitford reappeared with the registration for the motorcycle. He handed it to the officer and looked at me. "What's she still doing here? Aren't you going to arrest her for burning my garage?"

The officer examined the registration before glancing up. "She didn't do it."

"Bullshit." Brian sneered. "Marleen didn't do this alone."

"According to Miss Galloway, she did do it alone." The officer jotted notes on his clipboard. "She said her friend came to try to stop her."

"Right." Brian took two steps toward me and I struggled to my feet. His lips curled into a threatening grimace. "You did this. You hatched the whole plan and pulled Marleen into it. And now you're letting her take the fall for you?"

I shook my head, not in denial, but in rejection of his close presence. I wanted to back away, but I couldn't. The police officer had taken a half step forward. "Mr. Whitford--"

"Get away from my daughter." David strode up the driveway. I'd never seen anything safer than him at that moment. "You son-of-a-bitch, you stay away from her."

He caught me up in his arms as I ran toward him and suddenly the whole horrible evening rushed over me and I collapsed against him. I let him pull me against his chest. He smelled like aftershave, but I could smell my mother's perfume on him, too. I leaned into him and his arms closed around me like the best shelter in the world.

Brian backed away. "I didn't mean--"

"You meant to frighten her, you meant to threaten her, just like you did before." I heard a snarl in David's voice that surprised me. David was a peaceful guy. He took a breath, forcing his voice into a calmer timber, though his eyes never left Brian Whitford. "Can I take my daughter home, officer?"

"She's done here," the policeman said. "We'll call you if we need you to bring her in to the station tomorrow."

"You do that." With his arm around my shoulders he guided me down the driveway. I glanced back once just before we entered the crowd. The embers of the fire still glowed, silhouetting a fireman, Brian Whitford's slumped form and the policeman. I could even see a tiny maple tree sprouting from the gravel driveway at their feet. The policeman held out a piece of paper for Brian and Brian took a step forward to take it. As he did so, his foot crushed the tiny tree into the gravel.

David took me home that night and on the way I realized that maybe I hadn't accepted him as my father until recently, but he'd accepted me as his daughter ages ago. Maybe when he and my mom got married. Maybe when he first realized he loved her. Maybe even on that first ice cream trip in the middle of the night.

Mom said nothing when we got home. She hugged me, held me close just like she did with Dougie. Even Dougie, dressed in his pajamas and sucking on a bottle, came and threw his little arms around my legs, grinning up at me. I picked him up and Mom held us both. Then David came and put his arms around us, too.

The next morning, everything was very quiet when I got up. Mom sat at the table alone, and I sat next to her. "Good morning. Where are David and Dougie?"

"I sent them out to play." Mom sipped her coffee. "David took the day off. We thought we'd have a family picnic later. Maybe at the park."

"That would be nice," I said.

"Yes." When she didn't say anything else, I got a bowl of cereal and came to sit across from her in the breakfast nook. Mom looked directly into my eyes. "We thought we should celebrate your detective work."

"My detective work?" I choked a little on a spoonful of Lucky Charms. "I, uh--"

Mom shook her head. "Don't try to deny it, Charlie. You did a wonderful job finding out who killed Jeff. David doesn't think there's any doubt Brian will be arrested." She set her coffee cup down and leaned across the table. "And I'll strangle your thin little neck if you ever try something like that again."

I had no doubt she meant it. She sat back and folded her arms across her chest. "And don't think for a moment that I believe you weren't involved in Marleen's plan to burn down the garage, either. You say you rushed over to stop her, but you didn't seem in a big rush when you left here. In fact, you acted like you were waiting for something."

I looked down at my hands twisted in my lap. I didn't say anything for a while. Then I remembered the slip of paper with my father's name and address. "I drowned the paper." I raised my eyes hopefully.

Mom cast a surprised glance at the newspaper on the breakfast table. "What?"

"No, the paper with my father's name and address on it." I spoke quickly. "I made a paper boat and put it on it and set it afloat. It capsized and went down."

If you love something, set it free.

"Oh." Mom looked blank for a moment. "I'm glad. Maybe this means you've learned to trust me. What would you have done if the boat had come back to you?"

If it comes back to you, it's yours, if not, it was never meant to be.

I didn't have an answer for her.

That afternoon, Brian Whitford was arrested in connection with Jeff's death. The police called me in to tell my story, but to my relief they were more interested in my discovery of the motorcycle than they were in how I'd come to be at the Whitford place while the garage burned down. Because Brian couldn't come up with a suitable alibi for the night of Jeff's death, Marleen and I could testify as to his motive, and his motorcycle placed him at the scene of the crime, the district attorney didn't hesitate. Brian was charged with vehicular manslaughter and leaving the scene of the crime. Unfortunately, he had some money stashed away and hired a city lawyer who came out and plea bargained the charge down to second degree something or other. Brian spent eight months in jail, and then he came back to his parents' home only long enough to clean it out and sell it. The man who bought the house and garden behind it was an interesting character. He'd been in love with Mrs. Whitford long ago, and had been prevented from marrying her by her parents. A rich humanitarian, he donated the house and garden to the town to create the Sylvia Edwards Whitford Memorial Park.

That's where my story ends, but I think about the players in my own little tragedy often. I still miss Jeff sometimes. Although I've grown and changed, moved away from my old hometown and started a new life, I remember him as my first love, or perhaps something even more. Sometimes I almost think I hear his voice. It always turns out to be something else, though. My fiancé calling my name, a bird, the wind in the branches of an oak tree, a child's distant cry.

Marleen has changed a lot, and since that night I've recognized her as a true friend and Jeff's sister. She took full credit for burning Brian Whitford's garage, but the judge was lenient with her because of her past history with Brian and the fact that saving the motorcycle led to the arrest of her brother's murderer. The judge sent her to counseling and Marleen spent the rest of the summer and fall serving community service at the county library. Which worked out fine because she liked shelving books and straightening shelves and tables so much she got a job there after her community service was done.

Sydney Edward Moore remains in prison to this day. His lawyers have appealed the life sentence without parole that he was given multiple times…unsuccessfully. I have no idea if he killed Tracy or not. I know many in the black community still do not believe it. Yet because he was convicted and put in jail, his guilt is the only truth we know.

# Epilogue

I open the jewelry box. Inside, the silver chain with the Camaro charm shines dully in the sunlight. I haven't worn it since I left for college. Once or twice when I was home on break, I took it out to look at it and remember Jeff, but I never put it on. The links of the chain are cool in my fingers, but when I fasten the necklace around my neck, it warms quickly.

I'm out back by the pond when my cellular phone rings. It's Mom.

"Hello, darling," she says.

"Hi Mom." I watch a flock of ducks move gracefully across the pond. Turtles poke their heads out of the water. I can see one, just his eyes hovering above the waterline, his legs treading water. Turtles are beautiful things. I can't believe I used to throw sticks at them.

"Where are you?" Mom's voice calls me back to the present.

"Home, waiting for you." I glance over my shoulder. "Dougie's upstairs and from the sounds of it, he must have a couple of rock bands with him."

Mom laughs. "He's a teenage boy, dear. Don't you remember what they're like?"

Mom sounds so young. I know she has more lines on her face. I know she's 54 years old. But she sounds like she could be one of my friends, one of my peers. I smile. "I guess I'm getting too old."

"Have a kid or two. It'll benefit your perspective amazingly. Speaking of which, I've found the perfect place for you to get married."

"Mom!" I want to protest. I want to tell her to forget it. I know I won't. "You've got to be kidding me. I'm all set to order the invitations and you're still scoping out possible locations for the ceremony?"

I know I sound exasperated. I am. I love my mother deeply, but when she gets an idea into her head, it's hard to shake her out of it.

"Just meet me at the Whitford Garden." Her tone says she won't take no for answer.

"I can't get married at the Whitford Garden." This time I don't hesitate. I will not negotiate this.

"Of course not." She sounds like she's humoring me. "Just meet me there. C'mon, Charlie, let me feel like you at least have heard me out."

I sigh. "Fine. When?"

"Fifteen minutes. I'll bring you an iced tea." She sounds chipper all of a sudden. Obviously, she'd already decided I'd "humor" her. "It's your favorite iced tea--the sweet stuff from the Mrs. Rose's diner."

Mrs. Rose's diner has the best iced tea on the face of the planet. Mom knows my weakness for it. And so, for the second time that day, I find myself in Mrs. Whitford's garden, a place I'd sworn I'd never set foot in again. A breeze brushes past, pleasant and warm, and several people enjoying the day populate the garden. I sit on a bench commanding a view of both the rose garden and the mountains. I have to admit, although no huge changes have been made to the garden, the subtle differences make it lighter. A small army of volunteer gardeners weed and prune on a regular basis. Paths are neatly delineated. Several benches like the one I'm sitting on occupy shady spaces. I wonder why Brian Whitford's efforts never made much of a dent in the weeds of the garden. It's as if by removing him from the picture, the true nature of the garden has overcome the unpleasant feelings that had always haunted it.

The house still stands and has been renovated into a visitor's center. If I turn my head to the right, I'll see the spot where the garage once stood. Appropriately, it is now a parking lot. When I think of that night, I remember Brian Whitford's foot crushing the tiny tree more vividly than anything else. I wonder if he ever realized how destructive he really was.

Jeff sits next to me. "Hi."

"Hi." I've been expecting him. "I haven't seen you in a while."

"Nope." He leans back on the bench, still fifteen years old, frozen by death in a young, healthy, achingly beautiful form. "You haven't needed me. You resolved most of your problems when you burned Brian's garage down that night."

"Shhh!" I'm thirteen again, amazed that I've escaped without censure.

Jeff grins and shakes his head. "Don't think you got away with it. Your mom's too smart for that."

"You mean, since she knew I'd planned to meet Marleen, she knew Marleen wasn't the only responsible party, right?"

"Exactly." Jeff's grin fades and I feel the years pass rapidly so I'm thirty years old again. "So you're a crime reporter now."

"Yeah." I feel a little dizzy. "I think Tracy's murder got me interested in the legal process, but I didn't have the brains to become a lawyer."

"Bull. You've got plenty of brains. You always have." He pauses, his face a little sad. "You're getting married."

"Yes." It's the only thing to say.

"You love him?" I remember that Jeff's eyes are blue-green, like the sea.

"Yes." I do.

"How do you know?" Jeff sounds curious.

"I don't know." I shrug. "I guess because we laugh at the same things and always want to listen to the same songs on the radio. And when something makes me happy or sad, he always wants to know what it is. I guess I've always been sort of sentimental."

"No." Jeff shakes his head. "Your only problem was you believed in people too much. I guess crime reporting has beat that out of you, though."

"Not really." I pause for a moment and look out at the mountains. "It's funny how somebody can be convicted of a crime, but never really have anything to do with it."

"Yet if he didn't do it, he might as well have, because his guilt becomes the truth."

"Exactly." I look around me at the garden. "Like the way this garden used to be. There was light and dark and there were weeds and flowers, but there was no real distinction between them. The weeds grew over the paths and under the rose bushes. And there was darkness everywhere."

"It's not like that anymore, though." Jeff indicates a perfectly pruned rose bush without a weed anywhere near it. "Here there is only light and dark."

"Yeah." I sigh. "I sort of miss it the way it was, you know? I hated it that way, but I miss it."

"Nostalgia is often confused with homesickness. You aren't homesick, though. Not for here, anyway." He raises his eyebrows.

"No. Not for here." I close my eyes and think of my home on the coast, where light and dark don't mix. It's where I belong and when I go back, I'll be home again. As I'm thinking of this, the breeze lifts my hair and I feel Jeff's touch one last time.

“See how peaceful it is here?” I open my eyes and Mom stands in front of me, grasping two Styrofoam cups. She hands one to me. “And beautiful, too.” She sits next to me, in the space Jeff occupied just a moment ago. “Well, what do you think?”

I look around at the conglomeration of colors, light and shadow. I think of David and Dougie, two perfect roses and my wedding. I remember Jeff and Brian. And Marleen. She’ll be my maid of honor. How would she feel about coming back to this place? I think of Eric, my fiancé. He won’t care where we get married.

“Let’s just sit here for a while, Mom,” I say. “There’s a lot of memories here. Not all of them real pleasant.”

Mom sits in silence for a while. Then she nudges me. “Remember how you kids used to tease Mr. Whitford?”

“Tease?” I frown. “He was so mean. He chased us off if we so much as touched his fence. It always reminded me of the farmer in Peter Rabbit.”

“Mr. Magruder,” Mom says. “But old Mr. Whitford wouldn’t have hurt a hair on any of your heads. He loved kids.”

“Really?” I am startled. I remember Brian’s story about the belt with the spikes. I remember the barbed wire fence. And I realize Mom is rewriting my childhood again. Or maybe she is just superimposing her own truth over reality.

“Oh, sure.” Mom grins. “Rita Galloway and I used to laugh at the way he’d run at the fence when you kids tried to climb it. He always had a twinkle in his eye.”

"Right." I nod. "Okay. So he probably adored his son, too, right?"

"To the best of my knowledge." Mom lifts her shoulders and looks at me in a peculiar way. "Brian was always fed and clothed and went to school and college and everything. I don't think he and his father ever saw eye to eye, though."

"I wonder what happened to him." We're silent, each imagining a different fate for Brian Whitford. As we sit there, a cloud slides over the sun and I sit up, looking around at the garden. Every color in the rainbow and subtle shades between--all more obvious than ever in the dimmer light. Beauty only ever shows itself in the shadows. "I think you're right. I'd like to get married here. And David could come."

"Sure." Her smile falters. I know she's not sure David will be there, but I am. I'm sure he'll walk me down the aisle, and Jeff will stand beside the rose bushes.

## About the Author

Michelle Garren Flye is the award-winning romance author of five novels. Her most recent novel, *Where the Heart Lies,* has been described as an "engaging novel with charming and likable characters" and a story that "will make you believe in love and second chances."

Michelle placed third in the Hyperink Romance Writing Contest for her short story "Life After". Her short stories have been published by the romance anthology *Foreign Affairs,* Opium.com, SmokelongQuarterly.com and Flashquake.com. She has served on the editorial staffs of *Horror Library Volume 1, Horror Library Volume 3, Butcher Shop Quartet, Butcher Shop Quartet II* and *Tattered Souls.*

Michelle has a Bachelor's degree in Journalism and Mass Communication from the University of North Carolina at Chapel Hill and a Master's degree in Library and Information Science from the University of North Carolina at Greensboro. She is the mother of three and lives in North Carolina with her husband and their rapidly growing collection of pets.

**If you enjoyed this book, please consider posting a review on Amazon. I read all reviews and very much appreciate your comments.**

**Connect with Michelle Garren Flye online:**
Website: http://michellegflye.com
Facebook: https://www.facebook.com/pages/Michelle-Garren-Flye/132688623422175
Twitter: https://twitter.com/michellegflye

**Want more?**
**Praise for Michelle Garren Flye's other novels...**

**Ducks in a Row**

"Michelle Garren Flye does not hesitate to tackle some pretty uncomfortable subjects in Ducks in a Row. This well-written and thought-provoking novel provides a realistic look into how two people who love one another can find themselves on the verge of losing everything when they stop communicating and begin taking each other for granted."
-- Book Reviews and More by Kathy

**Where the Heart Lies**

"A romance with heart, heat, and a big ambitious story covering miles of emotional terrain. You'll be swept away."
-- Ellen Meister, author of The Other Life

"An ambitious and engrossing tale, full of complexities of both character and plot. Read this one on the beach, by the fire, in your bed... wherever. Just read it!"
-- Stephanie Stiles, author of Take It Like a Mom

"...a brilliant stroke of amazing and entertaining story telling."
-- Smitten with Reading

**Winter Solstice**

"...outstanding characters, wonderful storyline, great dialog, and delicious humor that just adds flavor to the story."
-- Booked Up Reviews

"The love scenes were exquisite and beautifully done."
-- The Romance Studio

"Well-written, with just enough sexual tension, plus believable conflicts that are finally solved satisfactorily."
-- Manic Readers

**Secrets of the Lotus**

"A glorious, sweeping love story packed with surprises. Brava to Michelle Garren Flye on her splendid debut."
-- Ellen Meister, author of THE SMART ONE

"...a delightful story with a confident heroine who is not afraid to be herself ... I found it difficult to tear myself away from this enchanting story."
-- Single Titles

"I would read this story, and any story by Michelle Garren Flye again in a heart beat."
-- Happily Ever After Reviews

"Sweet love story featuring a playboy billionaire who falls in love with a reporter. ... Very nicely written contemporary romance."
-- Romance Book Scene

"Michelle Garren Flye has successfully woven a modern day fairytale in her novel, Secrets of the Lotus."
-- Book Martini Reviews

www.ingramcontent.com/pod-product-compliance
Lightning Source LLC
LaVergne TN
LVHW050624100826
845148LV00011B/1722

* 9 7 8 0 6 1 5 7 9 1 5 7 9 *